PARIAHS

Maria Zaman

PARIAHS

Vanguard Press

VANGUARD PAPERBACK

© Copyright 2021
Maria Zaman

A CIP catalogue record for this title is
available from the British Library.

ISBN 978-1-80016-006-4

*Vanguard Press is an imprint of
Pegasus Elliot MacKenzie Publishers Ltd.*
www.pegasuspublishers.com

First Published in 2021

**Vanguard Press
Sheraton House Castle Park
Cambridge England**
Printed & Bound in Great Britain

Acknowledgements

A heartfelt thank you to all at Pegasus Elliot Mackenzie Publishers during this difficult period for their professionalism and perseverance regarding the fine tuning of my manuscript preparatory to publication. In particular, Vicky Gorry, Suzanne Mulvey, Elaine Wadsworth and Phil Clinker – for his diligent proof-reading – and to any and all who contributed behind the scenes to breathe life into this project. And finally, thanks go out to Pixabay, from where the cover image was sourced.

Prelude

The trials and tribulations of this lonely existence have been profuse and arduous. Too numerous to list and too distressing to recount. But this isn't about me, it never was. Instead, I invite you to walk with me as my journey draws to its inevitable conclusion and judge for yourself; pariah or liberator?

I will reveal what little I can in the time left remaining to me before... well, all will shortly be revealed. The little I can share with you is not out of any sense of egocentricity but simply because the memory of my journey leading to this point is vague, to say the least.

The knowledge I have accrued over the centuries is sacred and carried within my very soul, remembered over numerous lifetimes. It is a sense of knowing without being able to vocalise what it is I try to convey. It concerns the very nature of life itself and the continuance of spirit in all things. Some would call this religion — I am not one of those.

Many decades ago, or it could be centuries now — the passage of time is of no consequence to me now — myself and my co-conspirators conspired to bring about

His downfall and bring an end to His tyrannical reign over all dominions: in this life and the next.

Deemed a god — no, The God — by many. The Devil himself by an equal number of believers. Two facets of the same being, his mind fractured and unbalanced; who has ruled unchallenged since time immemorial, except by a brave few.

Guided by His callous hand, His minions have aided Him in the moulding of this world as He so desired. Without compassion or order, but purely for His entertainment and amusement. Casting down those who opposed Him, condemned to eternal damnation, and resurrecting those who blindly bow down to His will.

I was cast aside for my part in rallying dissension against Him. All knowledge of who I once was cruelly stripped from me. But He should have ended my life then — that was an oversight He shall live to regret. As with each new incarnation I remembered and retained a little more of who I was. Building this slow accumulation of knowledge over many lifetimes, sacrificing much as I rebuilt myself piece by inexorable piece.

As the world evolved in conjunction with humankind's ever-expanding technological advances, so my advancement increased in pace. The knowledge I sought having been made more freely accessible with the introduction of computers and the internet.

I have traversed the metaphysical nine circles of Hell and survived all the misery and horror that entailed. Losing my sanity on timeless occasions, the only way to truly find myself again. Utilising ancient methods of meditation and mind control to focus and strengthen my resolve and open my heart once more and receive the love of the Goddess.

Through all this and more I have endured, my goal — to locate and infiltrate God's darkest secret and those I seek, whose true identities elude me still. Imprisoned in the last place any sane soul would dare to look. But isn't that the nature of things when seeking that which is lost? And sane is not an adjective I would use to describe myself any more.

To any other, this place would seem impenetrable and therefore inescapable. A place of abject misery reserved for those pariahs that He fears the most. Those few souls who could still threaten His very existence. The potential of their accumulated power even in death was reason enough to spare them. Safer to incarcerate them and allow that knowledge to slowly dissipate and dissolve as their physical forms slowly wither and die.

Or so He foolishly believed.

I have no recollection of reaching this stage of my quest. This womb-like darkness that enshrouds me is absolute; even my footfalls create no sound as I descend ever deeper into the very bowels of this hell He has created. A place conceived to spurn the seekers of truth.

This forgotten, shunned place steals my senses, the seemingly endless spiral disorienting and distracting. But I would be wise not to nurture complacency here as He is omniscient.

I draw the outer garment tightly around me that I have purposefully worn for this my final challenge. A simple item of no magical significance, apparel of modern times — a hooded dressing gown, several sizes too large for my slight frame.

I sense your amusement at this, but aside from the little comfort and warmth it offers, its fundamental inclusion will soon become apparent to you — and hopefully to me; at this juncture, I'm as much in the dark as yourself. But to reveal too much too soon would be a fatal mistake. And to carry upon my person any items of power would only draw unwanted attention; therefore, the only power available to me is the knowledge I have compiled. It is my only weapon; it is all I need. That and my sense of humour, of course.

The claustrophobia this place cultivates tightens around me like monstrous psychic tentacles, constantly constricting and probing at my mind. I will myself to relax and allow the sensation to flow through me like cold winter rain, emptying my mind of all thought as I do so. My step never faltering, my innocence my only protection, and slowly the feeling eases off.

Sensitive to such things, I feel this place steeped in archaic magics, long forgotten — by most. And like vintage wines, they have now fermented into a powerful, heady brew. The resultant concoction not dissimilar to a tangle of spider silk, ready to receive and transmit even the most minor of magical conjurations. The vibrations conducted along those invisible highways back to their source; and I have no desire to confront Him and incur His wrath — at least not yet, because this is my pursuit and we shall play by my rules.

Finally, a faint glow of intermittent blue/white light permeates the darkness below, the fine hairs on the nape of my neck prickling in anticipation.

You would do well to quiet your breathing and hush your mind, constant companion, as a deadlier game you cannot conceive is shortly about to unfold, and I will need all my wits about me to emerge the victor. For if I fail, I will be condemned to spend an eternity in this void, this place out of time, erased utterly from history.

But no, I will not fail. I refuse to even contemplate the possibility. To even play host to such a notion could invite disaster. There is too much at stake and they deserve so much more than that.

Now that my destination hoves into view, my other senses are assaulted with an overwhelming sensory overload. And despite the smearing of menthol oil I have generously applied in and around my nostrils, the smell is still unmistakable. One that would not be misplaced in an abattoir and almost sends me reeling, accompanied by a foul acrid taste in my mouth;

sulphurous and acidic.

A low rumble also becomes discernible, one that seems to emanate through the stonework and caress the soles of my feet with a most unpleasant agitation.

With conviction, I enter this unholy place, this place of contradictions. It is both filled with light and seething darkness as the light tubes above strobe to and fro, and the room is both simultaneously uncomfortably hot and bone-numbingly cold.

The room is somewhere between a morgue and an abandoned psychiatric ward. The walls and floor paved with cracked ceramic tiles. The decidedly unsanitary state of the flooring making me instantly regret wearing my new moccasins, with faux lambswool interior.

And at the heart of this unhygienic nightmare a broad, cylindrical iron pillar plays host to a raging furnace. Kiln light reaches into the chamber through openings cut from the rusted metal, painting this place with a hellish wash.

Set at regular intervals around the chamber's circumference are the cell doors: steel grey and heavy. I quickly calculate eight, taking into account those set within the far wall and so obscured from my view.

I sense a movement in the far shadows as the guardian of this place makes itself known. Allowing me a moment for the pervasive atmosphere to soak in; one devoid of all joy, comfort and hope. A place for the truly forgotten. If you have ever visited Rhyl in recent years, you will know what I mean.

'It is indeed a great pleasure and privilege to finally play host to you after the passing of so many lifetimes.' The deep, sonorous voice echoes threateningly, heavily laced with the promise of the torments he is eager to bestow upon me. But I am indifferent to his threat, I am more prepared than he knows.

A shadow detaches itself from the gloom and a tall, emaciated figure stalks me, barely resembling the human he presumably once was. As a depiction of the reaper, I could barely conjure a better image myself. I am suitably impressed.

Unperturbed by my silence, the gaoler glides over to loom before me, the miasma of heat and flickering light animating his features most disturbingly. His claw-like hands and rictus grin twitch and spasm in the strobe-like effect.

His eyes... *his eyes*.

I avert my gaze and immerse myself in the perusal of the cell door on my right: the door lies ajar. My arrival was anticipated.

'I had feared that you had perhaps lost yourself during your long journey or succumbed to the many horrors and temptations along the way.'

Again, I fail to respond. The reference to my sanity and the multifarious pleasures of life is not lost on me. For in our own way, we are all saints and sinners, are we not?

The gaoler chuckles, the sound like dry stones rubbing together, at my stoicism; mistaking it for aphonic consternation.

The new word for today — aphonic, meaning mute. I firmly believe you should learn at least one new word every day. If you were aware of the meaning — as I'm sure you were — I'm impressed. If not, then I've saved you the bother of looking it up. A smiley face emoji at this point seems simultaneously inappropriate and appropriate: but perhaps not.

I throw back my hood defiantly in response and stand tall. This proves to be rather inadequate in light of my present company, as he towers above me. The darting shadow he intermittently casts crawls bleakly over my exposed skin.

I turn my head, lingering on the first occupied cell to my left, before craning my neck slightly further to confirm what I already know — the stairs by which I entered this place are gone; a blank wall now presents itself. This discovery is met with further merriment; he is beginning to enjoy my predicament a little too much. Now the bait is cast, I must be careful to lure him in.

He will be in no hurry to inter me. As he has already admitted, he has waited patiently for centuries for this moment. And he will want to plague me with unfathomable horrors and depravity first, providing him with fresh entertainment. The temptation will be irresistible for one such as he.

Or at least he can try.

'There is no escape from this place... even in death,' he reminds me as he moves towards the first sealed door.

The bait has been taken: let us then play — winner takes all.

And for any who may be interested, the vanishing of the staircase means nothing to me. I had no intention of leaving by that means anyway.

The shadows bloom and die in response to the unreliable lighting, revealing an altogether different creature before me as we reach the first cell door.

I suppress my shock at witnessing this monstrous metamorphosis — that was unexpected. The fragrant corpse that has now become my host and guide studies me for some reaction. But I grew up on a diet of zombie flicks; you'll have to do better than that. Unimpressed, I refocus my attention through the iron bars set within the square viewing window and the captive interred within this padded cell. The kind usually reserved for the criminally insane.

My heart picks up a gear as my breath catches in my throat, unprepared as I was for the sight before me.

Her six arms are splayed wide. Nailed through each palm and both ankles as she hangs inverted upon her specially constructed crucifix; which hangs suspended in the air, slowly rotating like a rotisserie.

Rivers of blood, blackened with age, obscure her

body as fresh rivulets glisten brightly like tributaries as they trace fresh trails even as I watch. Only her feet remain visibly blue-skinned, revealing to me her true essence.

Her eyes open briefly, the whites startling amidst this ocean of anguish. I feel ashamed at my self-pitying ways over the decades. I have no point of reference to even begin to conceive what she has endured.

I abruptly stand back and I have no need to assume my disgust and horror; it is quite genuine.

Possibly fuelled by my abhorrence or my lack of feedback regarding his previous form, the gaoler has yet again taken the opportunity to change guises: one more loathsome than the last, an abomination of the female form. The body lumpen and diseased, making her movements slow and ponderous as she shuffles towards her next exhibit, keen to nurture the disgust she has kindled within me.

She turns to leer at me as I follow at a respectful distance. Bones protrude from her glistening skin where none should protrude. I applaud the spectacle — internally — now this is more like it. And to complete the picture, a gobbet of thick, black ichor slides down her chin as she smiles a toothless smile and awaits me at the next cell door. A little clichéd perhaps, but her enthusiasm has to be appreciated at least.

I sidle up, playing my part as expected. She takes great pleasure in parading her repulsive nakedness. But

I have experienced Brighton beach during Britain's great heatwave of 2018 and have seen worse displayed in woefully inadequate bathing costumes.

I turn to peer through the bars to the accompaniment of a phlegmy chortle and inwardly cringe as her foul breath condenses on my cheek.

Somebody is in dire need of a mint!

But I have no alternative but to continue to play out this deadly game and I sense this latest form worn by the gaoler is particularly malicious and astute. I must be patient and dance carefully with this one, and remain aloof to her administrations.

My attention slides within this second room and a tasteless display of seventies psychedelia assaults my eyes. Orange floral wallpaper, discoloured with mildew, peels back like the skin of the fruit itself. The revolting linoleum, equal in bad taste and enthusiastically decorated with dried puddles and stains, I have no words to describe. But tastefully framed with an eye-watering price tag and I'm quite sure it would find a home in some suitably tasteless aristocratic vestibule.

The whole depraved scene is lit by a bare, low-wattage bulb suspended by a single cord.

A Seraph this time, unfettered, but her posture speaks of disillusionment, head hung low in defeat, her spirit broken. A once magnificent display of wings of light, dulled by centuries of neglect, stretch out at painful-looking angles. Possibly repressed or just atrophied in a similar way that muscles go after protracted periods of torpor.

I turn about as I feel the gaoler shift her position and find her gazing at a point opposite and slightly higher than the cell's barred window. Mounted there on the wall is a sword of exquisite craftsmanship. The weapon's once magnificent presence now tarnished by the passage of time. Perhaps in sympathy for its owner's present state?

I note that it is positioned in such a way as to make it visible to the imprisoned Seraph, should she ever care to elevate her gaze.

The gaoler subconsciously runs one bloated, festering hand across the glyphs etched into the heavy steel of the cell door, which until now I had overlooked. An added security precaution set in place for one who once served God himself. The gaoler's eyes still gazing almost lovingly at the sword as she does so. The dormant power that still resides within, casting some sort of spell over her. Desirous of this holy treasure, which had only been wielded in the name of all things righteous, but unable to touch it with her corrupted flesh.

Finally breaking the melancholic atmosphere, she, rather wistfully, endeavours to explain the Seraph's torment. Rather unnecessarily, I feel, but I must play to her desires and endure her proximity a little while longer.

'To gaze upon the one thing she desires, above all others. The one thing alone that has the power to release her, but being unable to cross the barrier that separates them is a torment beyond compare. Exquisite, don't you think?'

She turns to face me and again I decline to respond. The sword's allure over her still faintly evident, like a drug slowly dissolving in her bloodstream. But the effect is wearing off quickly and her eyes are filling with an unholy fervour. Reminiscent of that time in Amsterdam concerning the space cake, the German bank clerk and the kaleidoscope — now that was unholy fervour!

I take the advantage, while she is still slightly under the influence, and hasten to the next cell, never casting the sword a second glance as I do so. The gaoler would still be alert for that rather obvious play.

I quickly note the purity of the light held within the cell, one that does not spill out into the chamber beyond. Instinctually I realise this room is my final play and I continue casually on towards the next door. The gaoler taking this opportunity to transmogrify yet again.

The lumbering monstrosity that shuffles forward where I patiently await his arrival is that of an obese male. And judging by the excess weight he has gained, I may be waiting some time. Resembling something that has been badly stitched together by a group of drunken medical students for a bet.

I cross my arms impatiently and he sneers in response, not impressed by my outward indifference to his repugnant form. And make no mistake, this one is indeed foul beyond words. His beady black eyes twinkle in his doughy face as he finally arrives, and I immediately regret having not brought my handy travel-size deodorant.

'This is His favourite,' he confesses, licking his lips in a rather lascivious fashion. No doubt the same salacious seduction many a lucky girl has been subjected to on a quiet night out by many a self-professed Don Juan. But fortunately, his eagerness to show me not only His favourite but very obviously his own, too, has left the question of why I skipped the previous cell unasked.

I admittedly restrain my anger with the greatest of will now as I gaze upon "*his favourite*".

The cell is cast in the style of a medieval dungeon. The woman — stripped bare — is anchored to the stone via three heavy linked chains. Not enough slack available to her to even allow her to sit or kneel. Her beauty still evident despite her emaciation and long matted blonde tresses.

My empathic nature reaches out and briefly touches her pain as a cold blue eye fixes on my own as she senses my presence.

I feel the three manacles at the end of each chain, embedded in her flesh. Two encircle a rib each side, while the third encompasses her lower spine. The pain she is enduring is beyond my capacity to convey. Be thankful for that small mercy.

The sins of our Father. He will pay dearly for His trespasses.

The walls of her cell sprout numerous spikes, dark with rust or blood, and on each, a single skull is skewered.

The stench of fermented sweat is turned up a notch as the gaoler leans closer, conspiratorially. Perhaps fearing He will overhear what he has to impart.

'Each skull represents one of her sisterhood. Placed there when they were still fresh so she could savour their slow corruption. She being the last of her ilk.' He pauses.

Ilk? Who says ilk anymore? He really needs to get out more.

'But she will confess her secrets in time... for we have an infinity of time here.' He leans back, his disclosure complete.

Thank the goddess! I'm not sure how much longer I could have held my breath. But that was interesting: there are still some mysteries even He isn't cognizant to.

The gaoler's great girth means I have to circumnavigate his torso on my way to the final occupied cell. Meaning I have to pass close to the great iron furnace.

I feel my skin tighten in response to the intense heat. So, taking this perfectly placed opportunity, I slip from my dressing gown and drape it casually over one arm: confirming that the next two cells, proceeding my own — we shall see about that — are indeed empty. Which raises the questions: did the intended occupants meet with an altogether different sentence? Did they successfully evade that which was intended for them? Or are they dead?

I cast this final morbid thought aside as I about-turn and await the arrival of my would-be tormentor.

I am authentically taken aback at this next transformation — well, perhaps slightly; I have to give him/her points for effort.

What he has lost in girth he has gained in height, his appearance now brutish; like a blacksmith crossed with a professional wrestler. In fact, I'm sure I had a date with this one. One I had foolishly agreed to on a drunken night out. The following weekend brought home the sober reality of my mistake, though, and one swift drink was followed by a timely pre-arranged in-coming emergency call and a hasty exit.

If I had been aware of his true vocation then, I would have never agreed to meet up with him in the first place. And he had told me at the time he was in sales!

The next cell — focus, focus.

It is like peering into a crystal geode, the many mirrored facets seemingly having grown directly from floor, ceiling and walls, surrounding the woman who crouches at the centre: her palms pressed firmly over her eyes, a wild explosion of black knotted hair framing the image of her suffering.

Another woman? Strange that He should fear the power of the goddess so. But on reconsideration perhaps not so much. After all, highly emotional, intuitive states bear clear insight into the true motivations and intentions of others. And women of power, in particular, have been needlessly persecuted for centuries.

The countless reflective surfaces that imprison her are her reason for covering her sight, fearing she may catch a glimpse of herself. Although the temptation to do so and end her plight must have been overwhelming — although would He allow her that option? Probably not.

I step away and nod once in the direction of the cell I neglected earlier, and raise one enquiring eyebrow.

He steps aside to allow me passage, but the space is narrow and I am forced to brush against him, however briefly. An old play that one — I'm not impressed.

I press my face against the final set of vertical bars. The game is almost over, the prize is in sight.

The light within is pure and seductive and completely encircles its ebony core. Reminding me of a giant piece of frog spawn; although I'm quite sure that wasn't the look He was going for.

I push my free hand as far between the bars as it

will reach and stretch my fingers in a futile attempt to bathe them in this Heavenly light.

I hear the jangle of keys — success! The gaoler can't resist one final torment before I begin my long sentence. Or so he believes.

I retrieve my hand and stand back, inviting what I already know he intends. I remain calm and centred as he selects the appropriate key from the iron loop he has magicked from somewhere.

I quell my impatience as he seems to take an inordinately long time to select one key, considering he only has eight to choose from. Perhaps he should have also given deliberation into developing a brain as well as his muscular build during his last metamorphosis. A common oversight amongst his gender.

At last, the key is inserted, the lock is disengaged and the door swings inward on surprisingly silent hinges. I don't know why I expected the creak and screech of metal sorely in need of oil; too many clichéd horror flicks, I suspect. And at his rather chivalrous bequest, I step into the light.

I sense his bulk adequately filling the doorway behind me. I should engage caution now as this is the moment of truth; everything has led me to this exact moment in time.

I take a second cautious step, fully immersing myself. The light is invigorating and comforting and contradictorily deceitful and intimidating. An instrument used for centuries to deceive armies of faithful followers.

I catch a flitting movement within the stygian darkness and my eyes lock with a pair of smouldering red coals and I react quickly and decisively.

With a practised flick of my hand, I cast the garment I still possess across the barrier of light and take one step to the side as the dressing gown sails through the air and touches the darkness beyond. It is instantly snatched from the air and utterly consumed by what dwells therein.

I take a moment, however brief, to enjoy the varying expressions that flit across the gaoler's features: firstly, derision in reaction to my seemingly pointless performance; then rumination as he reconsiders his initial deduction. This in reaction to my own rather sardonic smile — I couldn't help myself at this point, his counteraction is so adorable. And lastly, fear, as the consequences of my action finally penetrate that thick skull of his.

All this transpires in mere moments as my final gambit plays out.

The spectral form streaks out of the darkness through the light — a dressing gown possessed with a deadly mission — at such velocity the only further reaction the gaoler can complete before impact is the dropping of his jaw. The collision, despite the gaoler's immense build — surprising even myself — carries him back into the main chamber, his feet leaving the ground completely.

A few seconds later, preceded by a rather nauseating tearing, choking soundtrack, his head re-enters the cell and lands with a wet slap on the floor and lies steaming in the light.

A single eyelid twitches in erratic accompaniment with one of his feet. A nice touch, I think, as I step over his corpse and retrieve the keys where they still hang in place.

Trying hard to ignore the shockingly large pool of blood gathering about his ravaged neck, which is difficult as the amount is indeed rather impressive, I focus on unlocking the cells as my newly freed accomplice retrieves the dormant sword from its mounting.

We will have to be swift now as the execution of His puppet will not be neglected for long.

As my comrade-in-arms crosses the fortified threshold, intending to reunite the former Seraph with her sword, I begin the task of releasing the crucified warrior from her bondage.

Whispered charms coax forth each deeply embedded nail; there is little need for stealth now. Pocketing one of the bloodied spikes as I complete my task, I then gently lower her as best I can to the floor.

Despite her period of disordered incarceration, she is as eager to leave her cell as I am to free the others and leave this place.

Once outside, she leans heavily against the outer wall of the chamber and waves me off: her strength and tenacity a sight to behold.

I make my way towards the crystalline cell, whilst the Seraph, now reunited with her sword, and recuperating fast, is accompanied by the shrouded figure — even with a prewash, that dressing gown is most definitely ruined — and together they enter the cell containing the chained woman.

The other raises her head as I approach, removing her hands as she does so, but her eyes remain firmly closed. I retrieve from a pocket the only other item I had dared to carry with me — a pair of mirrored sunglasses. The mundanity of this item, as I had hoped, was overlooked, their inclusion now apparent; my conscience haunting me until I finally relented and purchased a pair.

She flinches automatically as I gently slide the stems behind her ears, bestowing upon her the gift of sight once more, noticing as I do so that the price ticket is still attached — I'm glad I bought the expensive pair now.

She accepts my proffered hand and I guide her through the shards of reflective crystal to freedom. And despite her obvious weakness, she stands unaided; as do they all.

The blonde woman is now bundled in my bloodied

dressing gown, her chains severed by the sword, but I sense the iron loops still embedded within her flesh; these will be dealt with soon enough. Also, the demon is now revealed to me in all her shadowy glory; her fiery eyes effervescing with bloody revenge, her mouth smeared with the gaoler's dark blood.

Had she been drinking it? Well, that would explain the cocoon of divine light holding her in abeyance. But the gaoler's blood — gross!

United once more, they are gathered awaiting my direction, barely clothed in garments so soiled and tattered, to call them rags would be blasphemy in itself. We have no time to squander as I feel the atmosphere condense and the lights dim.

I lead my broken warriors to the cell intended for my sojourn and, brandishing the nail I retained, I scratch deeply into my palm — that one will sting in the morning and add yet another scar to my collection.

The blood flows brightly as I pump my fist to encourage the flow.

Then, reciting a magical incantation I have practised to perfection, I run my bloodied palm around the threshold of the room. Noting abstractedly that the gaoler has kindly furnished my otherwise stark cell with a chair. Granted it looks as if it was designed to carry a large electrical current — but still, how considerate.

The chair shimmers and dissolves before me as the blood sigil works its magic and opens a portal to another place: a place I recognise; a place of safety.

I stand aside and usher my friends through. The powerful conjuration I have just performed will assuredly evoke His immediate attention.

No sooner than this occurs to me, the furnace flares and the fluorescent tubing that has so valiantly tried to fill this cursed place with light finally gives up the proverbial ghost and simultaneously explode, showering the chamber with hot, sharp shards of glass.

Now my friends are safely relocated, I shake myself free from the psychic constraints I have swathed myself with: the freedom is intoxicating. And I form a message in my mind as I also step from this place to join them. A message specifically intended solely for Him. The words bold and exemplary as they breach the boundary between these two places before the portal finally seals for good.

And to you, constant companion, do not linger here; leave this place while you still can — I do not wish your fate on my already over-burdened conscience.

The game has played out to my satisfaction and a small determined smile plays on my lips as I deliver the message:

'Hear this, we are coming for you.'

1

Welcome back, it's good to see you heeded my advice and escaped that chamber of horrors intact; but of course, you did. A mere turn of the page later and here we are unified once more.

But for myself and my friends, in reality it has been almost a year since being consolidated and breaking out of that hellish prison. And yes, in case you're wondering, we did successfully administer our own sweet justice on one aforementioned deity — a complete and unequivocal success. The mission was completed rather *too* easily for my liking, though, and it has perturbed me ever since.

That nagging doubt has recently been proven not just to be my paranoia, as I will shortly reveal to you, together with the details regarding our confrontation with that deranged deity — all will be revealed in good time.

But for now, please be patient and allow me a little artistic licence as I unveil what has been and what is yet to come as we continue to expose this unfolding adventure together.

We've so much to catch up on since our return, it's

hard to know where to begin, and I have matured much since then. The time for dwelling on my past and of who I once was, and who I should be, is far behind me now. I am far too focused on being me, you might notice a few changes yourself, but it's all positive, I feel focused, content; or like content, as can be expected under present circumstances. But more on that later.

My crew, my team, my friends were in a woeful condition, both physically and mentally when first we were reunited. But warriors that they are, they were unanimous in the decision to take the fight directly to Him with all due haste. Their determination and performance far exceeded even my expectations under the circumstances. But since the aftermath of that long-overdue engagement, the healing process has been long and arduous.

At present we are somewhat fragmented. A cramped household of powerful warriors and goddesses proved untenable, as you can imagine. Fortunately, my more recent lifetimes saw the benefits of investing for many undetermined futures. And so, I wisely invested and accumulated a rather impressive financial endowment, which with a little manipulation I managed to bequeath to my future selves. And consequently, as well as being financially incumbent, I am also the proprietor of three substantial properties. An apartment in New York, overlooking Central Park; a rather spacious property situated in Kensington, London; and my favourite and current residence, a log cabin in Canada. You'll have to excuse me for not being more specific about exactly where in Canada. I know it's an expansive place, but I do cherish my privacy — well, at least I used to! And I'm rather understating the property when I say log cabin; it's more of a guest house really, located well off the beaten track, surrounded by miles of virgin forest.

So, my Canadian retreat was our obvious point of disembarkation when we returned. Space and privacy being the two deciding factors. At present myself, Mist — she of the chains, the last Valkyrie — with the power to determine who may die in battle and who may live — reside there.

I'm not so sure I'd be comfortable with that kind of responsibility, but it was obviously what He had desired, to rip that knowledge from her and use it for His nefarious ends. Previously, He had only been able to take another's life via the intervention of one of His many willing puppets. Fortunately, we thwarted that expedient as the consequences of such a plan, if successfully achieved, did not bear contemplating.

Mist had suffered most severely, and it is still evident, as she seems determined to single-handedly deforest the immediate area, as she spends an inordinately large percentage of her time felling and chopping them into manageable pieces for the wood burner; with the axe she salvaged from His trophy room and conveyed here.

Spoilers!

Don't get me wrong, I appreciate the gesture and I always found the whole process of wood chopping rather too physical and tedious; and if I'm being honest, I was loathed to harm the trees. Mist, on the other hand, has no compunction regarding their well-being. But the amount of kindling she has produced over recent months has become rather embarrassing. If I'd realised a few months ago her passion for lumberjacking, I would have suggested she begin construction on a small summer house. But a lithe but powerful six-foot Nordic beauty, wielding an unearthly axe with an ice-blue stare that would freeze anyone in their tracks — well, I thought best to leave well alone and let her work it out of her system. If there are sufficient trees in the forest, that is!

Next, we come to Maddie (but you may better know her as Medusa). If the Greek myths have any foundation in truth, cursed by Athena for desecrating one of her temples — she was raped by Poseidon there! Bit of a harsh judgement, that. But I haven't dared to ask her about that — would you? Some wounds are best left forgotten. And I can confirm that Perseus did not decapitate her; her head is still well and truly attached to her shoulders! I thought perhaps a name change would be beneficial, though, and she was surprisingly very obliging; perhaps it allowed her to move on from the past?

Nyx, on the other hand, wasn't. A deity revered by the ancient Greeks and the personification of night. Well, she wasn't about to take on a pseudonym and I wasn't going to argue with her.

I have to be honest, she does intimidate me a little. You can feel her aeons-old knowledge and power emanating from her, like standing too close to a furnace. Her complexion is as dark as a Nubian princess, and she does carry about her a certain regal air.

Her cheekbones and jawline are adorned with intricate designs that swirl and sweep below her neckline, and her irises are a breath-taking gold, her pupils a deep blood red that flares up when she is angered. Cursed by Him to crave living blood to exist, her teeth are shark-like and lethal-looking. But don't mention the word vampire in her company; don't even think it — in fact, forget I even mentioned it. And apparently, a curse cast upon a deity by another can't be reversed. This I found out from Maddie one night when Nyx was out feeding.

Anyway, these two have adapted to modern twenty-first-century life surprisingly well, apart from the odd glitch. I think it comes from age, experience and their inherent power. They have the ability to absorb knowledge from books, people (especially Nyx, literally!) and television; although I feel some of the information they have gleaned from that medium, hasn't been exactly beneficial.

The two of them hit it off, so to speak, and are living as my current New York tenants. And, believe it or not, run a tattoo parlour together! I know it seems unbelievable, but business is booming. Nyx turned out to be quite the artist, having taken to inscribing ancient designs directly onto the skin of her clients. Essentially permanently scarring her customers. I was concerned by this at first — health and safety issues, right? But she keeps the premises meticulously clean and, so far, nobody has contracted hepatitis or anything else for that matter, but I can't help but worry. But her clientele love her, and her unique work means that you have to book well in advance to secure an appointment.

Oh, and her eyes and pointy teeth: contacts and filing. If only they knew the truth. But this is New York, where the outlandish and obscure are just part of the culture there.

Then there's the issue of her dietary requirements. Fortunately, it is not something that she feels the necessity for on a nightly basis. Two or three times a month will suffice, and New York is infested with undesirables. At least I convinced her to focus her attentions on the more distasteful members of the community: rapists, murderers, drug dealers, you know the type. And I can't say I wasted much pity on them; the way I see it, she's performing a community service.

Now Maddie: her olive skin complemented by her

mirrored wrap-around golden shades and dreadlocks, the ends adorned with small golden snakeheads. It's a good look actually and has become integrated into the business; hair adornments. And where do the precious metals come from? Nyx's left-over meals. Drug dealers wear a lot of jewellery, and they decided it would be a shame to let it go to waste. And the bodies, ossified before the life leaves the body (apparently, she can only turn living things to stone), then dumped in the Hudson River.

As well as the tattoos and hair jewellery, Maddie does a nice side-line in ornaments. Fortunately, not people, but animals, which I can testify to, as I have a rather exquisite pair of raccoons on either side of the gate to my Canadian residence. And a rather impressive collection of stone mice in various poses. This irks me somewhat because I love animals; but I have to admit that a mouse-free kitchen is something I've dreamed about for years, and the raccoon's persistence in scattering my trash, despite the catches I've fixed to my bins, was becoming tedious. But I had to put my foot down after the addition of the bear statue in the back garden. Impressive as it is, it was just a step too far.

Anyway, her little stone effigies are causing quite a stir, and several images have already been posted online. How people marvel at the incredible detail! I just hope she doesn't get overly exuberant and start producing busts of wanted criminals. I have often wondered what would happen if you broke one open. Would it be just solid stone, or would the internal detail still be visible, like tree rings? There's a bigger part of me that just doesn't want to know. But the last time I dropped by to check up on them, there was talk of an exhibition of her work.

You can see why these two give me headaches.

Before I dash over to London, perhaps I should first explain a little more about Mist. Although I do worry about the publicity Maddie and Nyx are generating, it's probably a moot point now, considering it was Mist that first created quite an internet sensation, her story going viral across the globe.

Let me explain.

It was after we had returned to my rural retreat, victorious, via a portal I have permanently set up here. I keep it unlocked but secure, so animals can't just stumble through, but I suspect their instincts would prevent those kinds of incidents from occurring anyway; but it's best to be safe. I have them set up between all my properties — it saves a fortune in airfares. And it means I don't have to spill my blood to conjure up fresh ones every time. It's rather inconvenient, and painful, but I'm working on a way to circumvent self-mutilation, but portal casting is a relatively new craft to me and I'm still developing my skills.

So, Mist, as you will remember, still retained her

bonds. Of course you do; forgive me, I'm forgetting the time difference here.

Now, after their ordeal and conflict with Him, we returned immediately, but unsurprisingly nobody was in any physical condition to help her, including myself. Although I'm not confident any one of them could have offered any practical assistance anyway. And despite being quite adept in the manipulation of energies, I was still reluctant to attempt the removal of the iron bands. Her physical condition alone led me to believe that even the slightest misjudgement on my part could lead to further injury or even death. Yes, even goddesses can die under certain circumstances, and Mist was not looking healthy at all at this stage, and the dispatching of a goddess box was one I certainly didn't want to tick.

So, the only alternative then was to deliver her to the local hospital. I say local — it's a round trip of about a hundred and ten miles, give or take, in my old pick-up. So I sacrificed a little more blood — it was all in aid of a good cause, after all — and besides, my wound was still fresh after opening one up in that dungeon. So it wasn't so bad.

The plan then: leave the others to recuperate in my cabin after hurriedly showing them the basics: the fridge, the television (best to launch their education) and how a tap functioned. At least now they could eat and drink.

The story myself and Mist had concocted was this:

I, whilst in town picking up supplies, find Mist staggering along the pavement (still in my bloodied dressing-gown). I pick her up and take her to the hospital. That's essentially my part done.

Mist then claims she has no recollection of her abduction. Only that she was bound and gagged, bundled into a van and dumped at the side of the road. Her amnesia regarding her abduction, incarceration and her kidnapper's identity prevent her from giving the police any solid details. That included any particulars regarding her name, friends or family. Everything was essentially wiped clean. The police and doctors later put this down to shock, trauma and probably the use of a heavy narcotic or tranquilliser.

Simple, right? Yeah, okay!

The medical professionals were amazing. Compassionate, understanding, diligent and focused in light of this poor woman having been abducted and chained up, the rings still embedded in her flesh. It didn't even bear thinking about what had been inflicted upon her during her incarceration.

The three iron rings, in particular the one enclosing her lower spine, would require a long and arduous operation which only a highly-skilled surgeon could perform. And a very adept surgeon to insert them in the first place. If only they knew.

The circumstances called for the top professionals in their field, and they were flown in post-haste, all fees rescinded. I later realised that the publicity gained from the successful operation was probably worth far more than any consultancy fee anyway.

Initially, I have to admit it was a big weight off my shoulders as the doctors and nurses rallied round. I even reluctantly accepted their administrations regarding my bloodied palms, claiming I had fallen whilst carrying Mist.

Then the police arrived and the questions commenced.

Our simple pre-arranged stories held up and were accepted without question. What else could they do? It was plausible enough, after all. So then they became focused on the perpetrators of this heinous crime, and that's where our troubles began.

Firstly, came the dressing gown, which revealed traces of my DNA — a few strands of hair and flakes of skin (I don't have dandruff, by the way! But you know what these CSI people are like: meticulous). These samples soon mysteriously vanished, though. I may have employed a little magic regarding that misplaced evidence. But that was soon forgotten when it came to examining the dried blood. The forensics team were, in a word — flummoxed! This blood turned out to be not entirely human — no kidding, Sherlock! Anyway, I'm sure that will keep an army of boffins very busy for many years to come.

And, of course, I was only a concerned member of

the public, and Mist couldn't describe any of her captors anyway. And despite her being tested for several drugs and pronounced clear, it was accepted that any number of drugs could have been utilised that dispersed quickly in the bloodstream, leaving no trace.

The conclusion was that this was a highly organised gang of professionals that specialised in the abduction of women. Real scumbags.

So, as you can imagine, the media involvement from then on, in an attempt to secure some sort of lead from somewhere, was full-on. Had anyone spotted a suspicious vehicle on the night Mist was dumped? Was anyone seen acting suspiciously? Had anyone made any unusual purchases? Medical professionals within a two-hundred-mile radius were located and questioned.

You can imagine the kind of investigation that ensued.

The news channels broke the story about "the manacled-woman". Becoming quite impassioned, rousing the usually lethargic public to the plight of this poor abused woman. And by the time we left the hospital, not for almost two weeks — I hasten to add that even that was under great duress from the medical staff that Mist should remain and convalesce for a further period — the streets outside were festooned with news vans and reporters from all the major news broadcasters. Even several from overseas. I even recognised that woman from the BBC.

The media just lapped it up: it was the story of the year. Just what we didn't need.

And inevitably despite my best attempt to remain incognito — fat chance! — I was apprehended and interviewed on numerous occasions. But as I had very little information to disclose, they soon grew bored with me.

The operation itself was a complete success. The pressure that the surgeon must have been under considering half the world was awaiting the outcome doesn't bear thinking about. More than his career was at stake, I think. And unsurprisingly, no leads had been found, despite the intense investigation; and so Mist's abductors still remained at large, and by now the media and public were baying for somebody's blood. And I think at that stage it wouldn't have mattered whose it was.

On the plus side, Mist made a remarkable recovery; but she'll always bear those scars. And I'm sure there are still many more on the inside.

She despised all the attention, though, but she bore it with as much goodwill as she could muster. And it was as much as her cajoling me as my desire to be done with this media circus that set me to beleaguer the hospital staff into discharging her.

I had jumped back and forth between my home and the hospital frequently. Nobody even questioned the fact that I never appeared to have any transport. I had even opened up a small portal for my convenience, masking the hole at the hospital end, of course. You can never be too sure who might stumble across such enchantments; someone with a little magic in their veins might just feel something was out of place. And this usually quiet town was now filled to capacity, so I had to be extra cautious.

Eventually, I convinced them, promising Mist could stay at my home for the foreseeable future and that the surroundings would be conducive in aiding her full recovery; psychologically as well as physically.

Obviously, her memory hadn't yet returned and no-one had stepped forward claiming that this was their missing daughter or cherished wife. I think it was the rural setting my home offered that finally tilted the scales in our favour.

At last! I was exhausted, what with dodging the media, avoiding being seen jumping through portals and checking on the others back home as well. Those early weeks were trying, let me tell you.

So, trying to keep a low profile! Cover well and truly blown!

We still had to endure a handful of police visits and also one from the FBI, but we had nothing further to add. Although I did have to bundle the others off to London when the authorities arrived. A simple perception filter saw to it that the evidence of several lodgers wasn't displayed for all to see. But, finally, they declared they wouldn't trouble us again, and left us in peace.

So there you have it; we're quite famous now, for all the wrong reasons. But at least Mist's fully recovered, at least physically. I can hear the steady *thunk... thunk* from outside, as she splits wood. She definitely needs a new hobby.

Now, on to the others. Sophia — the Seraph. Well, why stay hidden now, considering the varying degrees of media coverage some of us had now received?

Her divine provenance allows her to easily disguise her true form, as angels have been doing for centuries to walk amongst us. There are still her angelic looks to be taken into consideration, though, and she turns many heads; male and female alike. So, it wasn't long before she walked into a modelling agency in London and her tall, leggy looks (I'm so jealous) meant she was signed up immediately. Despite all their adaptability to modern life and all that entails, it did take a little convincing on my part that the "angels" that modelled for a certain famous lingerie brand weren't real. Sometimes it's the simplest of things; with Nyx it's microwaves — it's like talking to a child.

But once the idea had formed in Sophia's head, there was no holding her back, and her unearthly beauty has now ensured her rapid ascension up the ladder, so to speak, and now all the top labels are desperate for her patronage. And I'm sure it won't be long, either, before she joins the ranks of those other "angels", and then perhaps the temptation to spread her six wings will be too much for her to contain.

I asked her about her six wings recently and she says the Seraphim have two pairs to cover their feet and face; it's something to do with humility in the presence of God. Well, little need for that veneration any more. And her wings are more a composition of light and not feathers; maybe that's just angels?

I believe she's in Paris at the moment and jetting across to Barcelona shortly afterwards.

I can feel that headache coming back!

There is one moment that still makes me smile; although it bears little relevance to my dialogue, I'll share it with you anyway.

I was in London with Sophia a few months ago now, in Regent Street. Acclimatising her to the intensity of the large city and simultaneously indulging in some clothes shopping. As they had all arrived at my home clad in rags, and as I'm rather petite my wardrobe was of little use, so much clothes shopping was endured. Don't get me wrong, I quite like shopping online, but when faced with a Seraph determined to dress only in lingerie, and trying to convince her that this wasn't socially acceptable and that she couldn't leave the shop dressed like that, the shop assistant being of no help whatsoever; well, that was an afternoon I have no wish to repeat. But considering how she looks in blue jeans,

I think she turns just as many heads as she would clad in dainty silks and lace.

Anyway, I'm getting off track. Regent Street, lots of heads turning — I'd like to think a few were turning my way as well — when a little girl of about four or five came to a halt directly in front of us, pulling her mum to a stop as she was holding her hand; her other was busy melting an orange lolly. She was in no hurry to be hauled off as she stood gawping up at Sophia, sticky orange running down her arm.

Sophia's social skills at this early stage were still a little awkward, to say the least.

'And who might you be?' she asked the little girl.

'Shawna.' She was all gap-toothed smile and sticky orange, unrelenting in her admiration of Sophia, despite mum's rather embarrassing attempts to pull Shawna away.

I have noticed that Sophia has that adoration effect on people, in particular children.

'I am Seraph,' she responded rather haughtily.

'Mummy, that lady's a giraffe,' Shawna pointed out to her mum, who, blushing with embarrassment, hauled her daughter away, mortified that she had called this tall, slender woman a giraffe.

The joke was lost on Sophia, and I made a poor attempt at concealing my mirth at the time. It wasn't until weeks later that she discovered what a giraffe was; for someone so divine, she can pitch a dark look when

47

she wants to.

Anyway, I digress, yet again. So, Maddie and Nyx in New York. Myself and Mist in Canada. Sophia, jetting all over the place to the fashion capitals of the world; so that leaves Kal by herself in London now Sophia has left. But, to be honest, she prefers her own company anyway.

I check on her frequently as the spells I have in place to conceal her six arms and blue complexion are complex and need constant renewal.

A true warrior is Kal, even in her human guise: pale-skinned with just the usual quota of arms, her well-muscled physique, though, commands respect, and it came as no surprise when I discovered she was teaching self-defence classes. She's good. I attended a couple, very energetic: I hurt for a week afterwards. She has gathered quite a lesbian fan club as well. In fact, she's the most approachable and down-to-earth out of all the team. I reckon it's something to do with her Asian origins, which you can make out in the cast of her eyes. She's all about the balancing of chakras, raising kundalini energy and meditation. Which is a large segment of what she teaches at her classes, balancing body and mind.

And yes, Kal — Kali — the Hindu goddess, destroyer of evil forces. You would never unravel her true identity on meeting her. She just has a certain way about her; people just instantly like her, myself included. Don't get me wrong, we're all one family now and I love them all equally; it's just sometimes the others can be such hard work. And Kal has created the least stir, although a certain amount of online social media coverage was inevitable regarding her classes; but that was the least of my worries — and I have a plethora of worries. Particularly since Mist and I received an unexpected visit from someone whose absence had been previously noted — remember the two empty cells? (Not including my own.) Turns out one was intended for some guy calling himself Jackson.

This was a few days ago, so I can now confirm he was genuine in his claim; he's quite cool, actually. But in light of what he brought to our door and our attention; well, the stress dial has been turned up to eleven!

I'll recount the event more or less how it unfolded, starting from when my "triggers" were sparked. I have numerous magical trip-wires set up around my property at a considerable distance — it gives me plenty of time to prepare for unwanted guests. They're a piece of cake to set up when you know how, and they don't react to the transgression of animals. Not any more anyway; the first few weeks after installation saw many sleepless nights, until I reconfigured the spell. I only have to renew them once a year — that's one of my first spring jobs, just when the rose-coloured trillium is in full bloom amongst the maple trees that supplant the pines on the periphery of my land.

Now, I was sceptical at first on hearing Jackson's story, but he's very convincing, if you like the rugged Clooney-look with a few years knocked off. I'm not saying I do; I'm not saying I don't. In fact, I've got a very open mind, and I'd be lying if I said I hadn't thrown a certain axe-wielding Valkyrie the occasional admiring glance. I'm getting off track here. What I'm trying to say is, this Jackson guy seemed like someone I could trust, and I have an instinct for seeing through people, and reading the truth.

But I'll let you make your own mind up on that score. I haven't forgotten my promise to relate the death of God, either; it sounds pretty ominous when I say it like that, but let's deal with Jackson first, as the incident is still fresh in my mind.

So, put your feet up; hey, grab a drink and some popcorn if you're so inclined, and I'll playback that event for you, the one that reveals the details of our forthcoming mission.

You know I knew that bringing Him down was just far too easy; at least now I have a better insight into why that actually was.

2

'Visitors?'

I glance up at Mist from where I'm sitting on the front porch, as she takes a respite from persecuting the trees to grace me with her presence. Dressed in tight blue denim and one of my old AC/DC T-shirts, looking every inch the rock chick — but with the addition of an axe. She takes it everywhere with her, like a child dragging around a teddy bear. She evens props it up next to her bed at night, not that she sleeps much.

'Four of them: two males, two females. Three are armed and one has abilities.'

Mist raises an eyebrow, impressed with my powers of foresight. I sensed them cross the boundary of my property fifteen minutes ago (I own a lot of the surrounding forest; I didn't want property developers buying up plots right next door). The magic trip-wires I set in place snapping, the feeling like hairs being plucked from my scalp. The one with powers causing violet flashes of colour in my mind's eye.

'Trouble?' she asks, tensing slightly, her grip tightening on the shaft of her axe.

I shake my head. 'I don't think so, but better be

prepared just in case, so stay frosty.' Who am I kidding? "Frosty" is her middle name. 'Wait here while I go and see what they want.'

I stand up and saunter down to the entrance of the property, where I await their imminent arrival, arms folded across my chest, flanked by my two stone raccoons.

Mist watches on, axe slung over one shoulder, ready to assist if the need arose.

It was a further five minutes until I could hear the deep rumble of the engine and a further two before I caught the first glints of sunlight reflecting off glass and the flash of matt-black steelwork amongst the dense foliage.

I made an attempt to psychically reach out towards the occupants of the vehicle, but I was thwarted — he had deployed his own psychic shields. Being cautious? Or hiding ulterior motives? So, beyond what I had already ascertained, I couldn't glean any further details except, judging by their mode of transport, they were definitely military.

The Humvee finally pulled up in a flurry of dust. The engine ticking as it cooled after the driver immediately switched off the ignition.

The occupants allowed the dust to clear before exiting the vehicle. Three of them at least, as the driver remained behind the wheel.

First to appear is Jackson from the front passenger

side, which suggests to me that he's possibly in charge of this little operation. He's definitely not military, and it's more than his appearance that convinces me; I can sense it as well, unlike the two that clamber out of the back.

The male, African-American by the looks of him and built like a safe. All muscle and no neck. Dressed in black fatigues with no visible military insignia, possibly special ops? He has an assault rifle casually hung from his shoulder. I don't like guns and its presence is duly noted.

The female is dressed in the same unambiguous uniform and is similarly armed. Her long, straight black hair is drawn back tightly and secured into a ponytail, her eyes are dark and attentive.

She'd probably get on well with Mist — she has that aura about her, one that says, "mess with me and I'll snap you in half!" And she wouldn't look out of place wielding an axe, either.

Hey, we could start a band! I've always fostered that dream, and fancied myself as a singer.

It also looks from here that she has a prosthetic arm or at least a hand, and not a standard one fit for public consumption, either; this looks more like Tony Stark tech. Okay, so these guys were serious and well connected.

Jackson, as I was soon to discover, indicates to his two escorts with a nod that they should remain by the vehicle, before he walks over to meet me.

'The name's Jackson.'

That was quick. I didn't expect him to be so forthcoming.

'This time around,' I respond.

He laughs and I know instantly that he's cottoned on. Yes, he's got magical talents all right. A bit different to mine, though. I sense he has powerful telepathic and telekinetic abilities. I'm not entirely without my own, but they're very latent; my talents lie elsewhere. He interests me, and not just because of his good looks; I'm trying to approach this situation from a purely professional angle.

Like myself, he's had numerous remembered lives. And I'm recalling more and more details since I've been reunited with my team. Anyway, you have to learn to constantly reinvent yourself; it gets to the stage that a name means nothing, it's just a word you respond to. So, Jackson is just his latest persona.

'Yeah, this time around,' he agrees, smiling, one eyebrow raised quizzically.

He's got a nice smile. I try not to smile back; this is potentially a serious situation and I'm not letting my guard down yet.

'You've changed your hair colour.'

What? Dammit, he's obviously aware of my own and Mist's brief period of fame; no surprise there. I dyed my hair black in a vain attempt at disguising my identity from the reporters that still lingered in the local town and accosted me from time to time when I had to shop.

'I'm Alice.' Like he doesn't know already, but I couldn't very well give the police a false name. Besides, it's about time I properly introduced myself.

'Hello, Alice, this time around. Are you going to invite me in?'

'That depends? Does that include your armed associates as well? Because I get a little inhospitable when there are guns involved.' I peer around him, indicating his loitering colleagues. Despite his friendly demeanour and open mind, I've got more than just myself to consider here. 'And if you tell me what this is all about, I'll think about it.'

His expression goes all serious: the smile is dropped and his eyes look deep into mine and I'm instantly reminded of the encounter with Him. Just what exactly does this guy know?

He breaks eye contact and glances back over his shoulder. 'Don't worry about them; this is a joint military and well... how can I put it? Enhanced operation? But I'm in charge here.'

Is he? I get the strong impression he is, and enhanced? So, he's letting details slip intentionally; he's reaching out to me. But his answer also raises more questions, like who exactly is he commanding? And are there more stationed in the local town? Not nearby, at least, as I'd certainly sense them.

Well, I may look like an unprepossessing petite thirty-year-old, which, essentially, I am on the outside, but I'm not, and these folks are trespassing and the guns are making me nervous.

'I don't like them either,' he answers my thoughts. 'Guns, I mean,' he clarifies. 'I much prefer other methods,' he adds.

Didn't expect that, I should have; his telepathy is good — I didn't even notice him in there. And I could misconstrue that last comment as a lightly veiled threat.

But it's time to cut to the quick. 'Are we talking about magical abilities here?' Okay, answer that one honestly. If he does, then we can talk; but if he deceives me in any way, then he and his friends can quit my property. I might even allow Mist to put her axe through that expensive-looking chassis.

He takes a moment and scratches at the back of his head. Is that some sort of coded signal, or am I just being paranoid now? He finally lets out a deep sigh and shrugs.

Okay, here it comes, what's it to be?

'I know about the others; not just Mist, but all of them.'

I don't answer; he could have gleaned that information off the internet. Besides, he might not know about *all* the others.

'I know what you accomplished. The breakout, the confrontation with Him. I know everything.'

Right, I have to admit that's left me rather speechless. I wanted a bit of honesty here, but I didn't expect that. He takes advantage of my silence to continue.

'One of those empty cells was intended for me.'

'And how exactly did you avoid your incarceration?'

'Same as you — magic, if you feel more comfortable with that word; I prefer to use the term metaphysical intelligence. Constantly reinventing myself, always on the move and never settling down for any lengthy period. Not becoming emotionally attached to people. Learning, adapting, developing my skills. Sound familiar?'

'Sounds about right,' I agree. 'Were you aware of that place before I broke in and out, or after?' I'm genuinely curious now.

'Before, but you didn't break in; you were allowed in.'

I have to admit I'd harboured that thought myself.

'I've been keeping an eye on you — a psychic one, so to speak. I haven't been following you or anything like that. You know, via the aether; I don't know exactly how you refer to it.'

Aether — that's good enough. Essentially, the spiritual plane where all my conjurations are manifested. Visualise several thin transparent layers sandwiched together. If you look at them square on, it appears to be a window, for want of a better description. It's only when you view it from a different angle, and with scrutiny and practice, that you can make out the individual layers. The source of all things outré: magic; psychic abilities; spirit manifestations and ultra-terrestrials, if you believe in that kind of thing. Or they used to dwell there; most have now been exterminated over the centuries. His minions took care of that.

I just nod, encouraging him to continue.

'My skills differ considerably from yours, and although I was probably able to enter that place, I didn't possess the skills to create an escape route. Then you'd have had the task of rescuing me as well, and that would have left you vulnerable to attack from a certain other...'

He tails off, struggling to find the right word. What the hell, I've left him floundering long enough. Besides, what he's saying resonates deep within me.

'This isn't over yet, is it? He was just the start, wasn't He?'

He nods, relieved I've stepped in.

'And you've been, what, protecting me from whoever this other is? What, like a guardian angel?'

'Yes.'

'How?'

'Deception. If you don't want someone to read your thoughts, then you learn to develop different layers of thought. Then cast them out like nets. It confuses and misdirects.'

'So, you've been casting nets around me?' I was struggling to come to grips with this concept. Why hadn't I detected them over the years? Unless he was really that good.

'Not around you, but around those who sought you. Or at least the ones manipulated by Her. But Her powers are weak in this realm and I've got quite good at it over the centuries.'

Her? What, God had a wife, is that it? I should've guessed.

'But why put so much effort into covering for me?'

'Because you were important. Without you, your friends would still be locked away, forgotten.'

This is the most revealing conversation I've had with anyone, like ever. And I can recall a couple of images I'd stumbled across online recently — well, I don't know if "stumbled" is the right word. I don't believe in coincidence. You know, those creature pics that turn up now and then of someone wrapped up in a fur coat claiming its proof of Bigfoot, or a poor diseased hairless monkey someone proclaims to be indisputable proof that aliens are amongst us? You just know they're fakes, but still, that tiny part at the back of your mind still thinks "but what if...?" I'm getting a horrible feeling about all this.

'And we need them, why?' I point out his patiently waiting friends.

'We're going to need as much help as we can pool together; and besides, they're more informed than you know. They've been called upon to deal with a few, how shall I put it…?'

'Monsters?' I ask.

'Yeah, okay, monsters,' he agrees.

Those images were real! I should really learn to trust my first instincts when it comes to things like that.

'And these "monsters" are susceptible to bullets, then?'

'Fortunately, yes. Although the bigger ones require something that packs a little more punch.'

'And how exactly did you become involved with the military?'

'Special ops, to be exact. They operate outwith the jurisdiction of the regular army, and they came to me. I was a professor at Cambridge. Taught English Literature, but I had an interest in cryptozoology as well, a little side-line.'

'You manipulated them into seeking you out and recruiting you, didn't you?' I'm impressed.

He nods. 'But don't tell anyone.'

'How bad are things?'

'These monsters, demons, whatever you want to call them, are appearing in alarming numbers. The reports have increased from one or two a year over the last couple of decades, ones that we can at least identify and confirm have a direct correlation to our particular problem. This year alone we have identified over fifty and had direct contact with twenty-two. Some are destroyed by locals, burned mainly, some just disappear before we can deploy a team to subdue it. Things are getting out of hand: as fast as we try to shut down sites and remove images, someone else is posting more. And they're good at evading us; we just don't have the resources or IT skills, to be honest, to keep on top of the situation. If this spirals out of control, people are going to start to panic. The last thing we need is one of these things to appear right in the middle of Times Square or Piccadilly Circus.'

I imagine the ensuing chaos and recall those images online. That bad feeling is getting worse. You know when you've eaten something off and you know the inevitable is going to happen? But you're just not sure from which direction disaster is going to strike.

'Who's this She, you mentioned? Is She behind all this?'

'God's better half, for want of a better description. And yes, She probably is behind this. It would be logical to assume that God had a counterpart.'

'Yes, that's what I'm thinking, although it didn't occur to me at the time. You know where She's located?'

'Can't give you exact details on that, but we've unearthed a doorway and we have a guide.'

'A guide?'

'The final member of the team. The eighth cell.'

He knows her, or of her. 'Where is she?'

'Not currently a resident in this realm. Never was; she was cast out. From what I've managed to gather, She had a part to play in the judgement upon the rest of your team, but She refused to relinquish Her hold over this one. I can only assume that it's because she is a guide to the newly dead; well, those who die in sacrifice. I'll explain it in more detail later, and we've got intel that suggests that these creatures are more human than they appear. There's a definite connection. I think She's been planning this for aeons. But I've kept contact to a bare minimum in case I was detected.'

'How did you first make contact?'

'By extreme methods.' He rolls up his sleeves slightly to reveal three parallel scars on each of his forearms.

I take an involuntary sharp intake of breath. This guy has experienced some dark times.

'The burden of what I knew became too much to bear over the years and well...' He shrugs. 'And perhaps that's how it was always meant to be; we made contact, and she sent me back with a greater understanding. And we've maintained a certain psychic link ever since.'

'You trust her?'

'Yes.'

Okay, I'm buying it. I sense his mind is open and

so is his heart chakra — Kal helped me develop that little skill, and it's proved useful. And magic is about the mind and heart. An open heart is important: it keeps you on the right path and keeps the darker elements at bay.

'What's her name?'

'Ix-tab.' He pronounces it eesh-tab. 'Some Mayan refer to her as the lady of the rope, as in the hangman's noose. Her existence was always a matter of conjecture amongst historians, and now we know why.'

'She was kidnapped by Her.'

'In a manner of speaking, yes.'

The hair prickles on the nape of my neck as Jackson relates this information and I hear her name uttered: the missing eighth member of our team.

'Well, you'd better come in, then,' I suggest; besides, I just heard Mist planting her axe in my porch in frustration, so we had better include her in proceedings before my rocking chair makes it to the kindling shed.

'Is it okay, too…?' He indicates his crew.

'As long as they leave their weapons outside.'

'Your friend with the axe going to be okay about that?'

'As long as the bionic woman remembers her manners.'

Jackson gives them a prearranged signal and they stow their weapons in the Humvee, including a handgun each they had holstered, before coming to join us.

'This is Corporal Belyakov and this is Sergeant Jones.'

I acknowledge each with a nod.

'I just need to grab a few documents.' Jackson nips back to the vehicle and a disembodied hand thrusts a manilla envelope out of the driver's window for him.

'Your driver be okay out here?' I ask.

'She'll be fine,' Corporal Belyakov answers, her accent as Russian as her name suggests.

I shrug, whatever, and I lead them back to the house.

'I like your raccoons,' Belyakov comments.

'Thanks, but wait till you get a load of the bear in the back garden.'

3

With cold drinks dispensed and everyone settled comfortably in the spacious, airy living room, Jackson finally prepares to reveal the contents of that envelope.

As it turned out, Mist had overheard enough of the conversation to get the gist of what was unfolding. I had no secrets from her anyway; I just had to verify Jackson's authenticity before allowing him in.

She'd taken the single-seat positioned opposite the three visitors, her axe leant against the arm-rest, as she cast her icy blue stare over them warily.

'Before we begin, I'd better introduce myself properly,' Jackson informs Mist.

'I know, it's Jackson, I heard. And you are Belyakov and you are Jones.' She glares at them each in turn. 'Mist.' She simply states her name.

There, well, that's the introductions over with.

'Anastassia will suffice.'

I note Jones doesn't volunteer his first name. Or maybe that is his first name?

'I like your T-shirt,' Anastassia comments, referring to Mist's choice of top.

'I like your arm,' Mist responds.

Anastassia rolls up her sleeve to reveal the extent of her prosthetic, which extends right to her elbow. It appears to be constructed from a flexible metallic substance. Clear segments display a myriad of pulsing, light-emitting diodes beneath, instead of bone and muscle.

Mist nods appreciatively. 'It is the arm of a warrior.'

'I like your axe, very unique.'

What's going on here? Have these two just become best friends? When did that happen exactly? In a rather cold, detached, emotionless kind of way, that is. They'll be out the back next chopping wood together, exchanging lumberjack anecdotes!

'Where did you get that, Stark Industries?' I let my smile slip at my little attempt at humour, as it is met with an icy glare and an equally dark look from Anastassia.

'We have our contacts,' Jackson responds vaguely, and takes a sip of water before proceeding to display the images contained within the envelope on the coffee table.

I don't drink coffee, I drink tea, so what is it with calling them coffee tables? An ingrained habit, I guess, but if I'd have called it a tea table, you probably would have thought "what's that?" I'm sorry I'm rambling now — those images fanned out before me have set my pulse racing.

'I lost my arm to one of those creatures.' Anastassia

indicates the pictures laid out before us, each glossy image displaying beasts, not of this world, or any world; these things just shouldn't be. 'Bit it off clean at the elbow,' she concludes.

'I'm sorry.' Not very original, I know, but what do you say to someone who has had their arm bitten off by a demon?

'These things are to be expected.' She shrugs, rolling down her sleeve again.

'The battlefield is no place for weakness or regret,' Mist adds.

Anastassia nods in acceptance of her words and picks up a glass of water delicately with her bionic hand and sips at the cool liquid meaningfully, as if trying to prove a point that is completely lost on me.

Resisting the urge to suggest that the two of them go out and play with the axe while the adults talked, I instead turn to Jackson, as I can sense he has further details to reveal about those images.

'You mentioned earlier that some of these creatures contained human DNA?'

'Yes.' He takes another sip of water before continuing. 'Six years ago.' He fishes out a particular photograph that shows the image of something resembling a crab or a spider which also possesses a face, a rather human-looking face.

'This creature was reported to the local authorities in a small village in Bavaria. At first, as you would expect, it was initially disregarded as a hoax, until someone had the foresight to photograph it.'

That would explain the slightly out-of-focus amateurish shot. I pluck the image from him to study it in closer detail.

'I know what you're thinking,' he says, as I look at him, a frown on my brow. 'We can confirm that the face is indeed human. The picture has been verified as authentic. It certainly left the experts mystified.'

'Did anyone question the person who took this?' I pass the photograph across to Mist as I ask.

'He didn't survive. A search party discovered his remains and his phone. There wasn't much left of him. Four months later, police in Edinburgh, Scotland, were called out to an incident in the city centre. Someone called in to report that their friend had been dragged off by some kind of animal.'

'No other witnesses?' Mist asks, tossing the picture back on the table and selecting another.

'The incident took place just after four in the morning. The person who made the call was sufficiently inebriated that the police doubted that the story held any concrete fact. Until they searched the immediate area. They found her butchered, and the coroner had to rely on dental records to identify the victim.'

Mist had already identified the incident shots of the victim and was frowning in consternation.

'What happened to the creature?' I ask, catching a

glimpse of the image in Mist's hands. I don't want to see any more.

'Vanished. No trace whatsoever.'

'Then how can you be so sure that these deaths are connected?' Mist holds up the image and I discreetly avert my eyes and take a quick sip of water to moisten my mouth, which has suddenly gone very dry.

'Since those two incidents and now, the most recently we've become aware of was last week: various reports have been received regarding creatures from across the globe. Many corroborated by photographic evidence. Ireland; Belarus; China; Brazil; Egypt; the States. The list goes on. Ninety-four to date, and they're just the ones we can verify.

'So far we've managed to intercept and suppress the majority of the images and videos posted online. The few that did elude our team were debunked as fakes, which has been largely successful. But we're fighting a losing battle; these manifestations are increasing in number. This story is going to break soon, and if the news channels get hold of this…'

I cast my eyes over the gruesome display of shots in both colour and black and white as I digest this information. I won't go into detail, in case you're snacking, but I do recognise one image and I pluck it from the carnage.

'This one' — I hold it up — 'I saw this online a few months ago.' A real horror pic — Clive Barker eat your heart out — sorry, but I have to share this one with you. Suspended between two walls in what looks like an alleyway, judging by the dumpsters and piles of discarded rubbish in the shot, is, or was, something that is recognisably human — just.

Its flesh is stretched and torn where the skeletal structure has burst forth and grown into long shards, jutting out from elbows, knees, ribcage and spine. These extensions are embedded in the brickwork, holding it in position several metres above the ground. The white of the bone streaked heavily with blood, the wounds where it protrudes are raw and ragged. The clarity of the shot shows the face in sharp detail. Human, female, and suffering indescribable anguish.

Jackson nods solemnly. 'That was taken in Detroit. It took eight cops and a lot of ammunition to bring it down. Two of the cops lost their lives, four more are still in therapy. Our team quickly responded and took possession of the remains.'

'I take it you have a large team?' It seems a bit of a stretch that these three could react so quickly to such a situation.

'We are working in conjunction with military and police across the globe to try to contain this,' Jones explains.

I almost forgot Jones was here; I was beginning to think he was mute.

'You still have the remains?'

'Cremated,' Anastassia confirms.

Jones must have used up his quota of air time.

'And what did you find out?'

'Not much.' Jackson shrugs apologetically. 'Except we did establish the identity of the victim. A Mrs Elizabeth Forsyth, formerly of 6 Chambers Close, Exeter. She had recently died of cancer. We have a death certificate.'

Note to self: scratch Exeter off my places to visit list.

'So, all of these…'

I lean forward and spread out the photographs further, catching glimpses of things I cannot now unsee. In particular, the diced-up remains of the people who fell victim to these creatures — like Jackson Pollock meets Jack the Ripper. Instead, I shift my eyes to the shots of the creatures; loathe as I am to study them further, I need to be fully aware of what we're dealing with here.

One looks like it's been turned inside out, eyes peering out of a ruptured ribcage. Something bear-like, but I use "*bear*" in the vaguest sense of the word. As it has far too many teeth and not where they're supposed to be. And a creature that would look more at home in the ocean, covered in tentacles tipped with child-like hands.

'… used to be people?' I finally conclude, a little distraught, I must admit.

'That one' — Jackson points out the one I have just described — 'was found washed up on a beach in South Africa. And yes, *used* to be human.'

'What's happening?' I am admittedly bereft of a witty riposte for once.

'We were hoping you might have a little insight. The only theory we can formulate is that they're being sent here with the intention of a full-blown invasion. Ix did suggest to me that these creatures were tearing their way into our reality to possibly escape.'

'Escape from what?' Mist asks, sitting forward, her cool gaze fixed on Jackson.

'His better half,' I add for Mist's benefit.

'Well, that's what I'm proposing we find out,' Jackson affixes.

'We? You mean a one-way trip to hell, essentially?' I'm not overly enthusiastic.

'Well, I was intending on coming back.'

'So, all we've got is possibly God's counterpart, possibly His wife, is behind this and you're planning a little foray to the underworld to locate and dispatch Her. If that is what is behind these creature mutations, that is. Sounds like fun.' It doesn't in the slightest.

'Basically.' He nods.

'Then what alternative do we have?' Mist seems committed anyway.

'I mentioned before that I believed you had been allowed to enter that dungeon,' he continues. 'And you admitted that His execution was easier than you had anticipated.'

Mist nods thoughtfully, before speaking for us both. 'It was as if He wanted us to slay Him. As if He loathed what He had become. Sophia told me that He was once a force for all things good. She alone could testify to that. Someone or something tainted Him, infected Him. Perhaps it was only His divine power and knowledge that held the poison in abeyance for so long, slowly eating away at Him and corrupting Him.' She glances over at me and a sudden flash of inspiration passes between us.

'Of course, it all makes such obvious sense now. Despite your incarceration, in a way, He was protecting you and the others, until the time was right. Until then, He had to show willing and comply, be seen to be the willing accomplice and tyrant.' I cast Mist an apologetic look. I know how much she suffered and it still pains me. But if He had shown anything less towards His charges, then perhaps the outcome might have been so much worse. 'And only I could successfully penetrate those barriers He had installed and successfully escape again. So, my freedom was necessary to accomplish this.'

'As was mine to ensure you continued to remain so,' Jackson finishes.

'So, He was being cruel to be kind?' Anastassia asks a little sceptically.

'You have no idea of the torments He committed upon myself and the others,' Mist informs her.

Anastassia reaches across the table and clasps Mist's hand. 'We shall avenge the crimes committed against you together.'

What? Don't I get a say in all this, or are the sisters of mercy going to do this all by themselves? Just the two of them? But I do feel ashamed; it has haunted me ever since I rescued all five of them. The truth is, myself and Jackson were granted our freedom it seems while the others endured centuries of torment and pain I can't possibly conceive of. Although I have suffered in other ways, and so indeed has Jackson: those scars he wears are testament to that. But it is small solace.

'Quite recently, last year, in fact…'

We all turn our attention towards Jackson as he steers the conversation elsewhere.

'… a manuscript was unearthed in the vaults beneath the Vatican.'

I'm impressed; how did he get in there? You know what I'm going to ask, and I can probably guess what the answer's going to be.

'How did you get access down there?'

'We initiated communication with the Pope and, in light of recent events, they were very co-operative.'

Okay, more detail than I'd anticipated. So, the Vatican was in the picture as well.

'This manuscript was only a copy of the original,

but it dated back to 2700BC. In it was revealed the details about, "*that which was hidden beyond the sight of all but God. Entombed within hell's heart lay God's great secret — His warriors*" — was exactly how it translated. Who, when the time came, would "*rise-up and sear the darkness that would descend upon the Earth and re-establish the sacred order?*" Pretty much what it said; the language was obscure, but you get the gist.'

'So, what exactly can you bring to the team? Except for translating ancient texts?' Mist is still rather resentful of Jackson; at least I broke her out, and that counts for something at least.

'I have other talents.'

Mist just raises an eyebrow somewhat scathingly.

Sometimes she doesn't speak much, but she can convey volumes with those eyes and brows.

'I have maintained contact with Ix, who I've already mentioned. Of whom Alice knows a little more.'

He's on first-name terms with her? And he pronounces it Ix as in Nyx without the N. What's with that? That wasn't a little bit of jealousy nibbling away at you, was it, Alice? I've only just met him! And here I am reacting like some immature schoolgirl. Pull yourself together! This isn't the time or the place.

Mist gives me an inquisitive look and I give her a frown in return as she detects my concentration deviating off-track.

Jackson continues, heedless of our muted exchange. 'A Mayan deity, interred in a purgatorial realm between this world and the next. She has endured the company of the recently dead that walk the thin line between sane and insane for centuries. And the pressure placed upon her has increased substantially over the decades as suicide rates increase at a rather alarming speed. Hers has been an existence burdened with unending pain, misery, suffering and death. Since our contact, about twenty-five years ago now, I have attempted to alleviate her affliction; and in turn, I have suffered as a consequence. I know what it is to endure the sweet misery of loneliness and walk the line between life and death; but granted neither, it is a heavy burden.'

'Then she is a sister to us.'

Mist still isn't letting him in, but I'll just have to give her time. She has suffered at the hands of men, or the form that loathsome gaoler donned at least, and I can understand her reluctance to just blindly accept this stranger in her midst; particularly a male. But she appears a little mollified now after poking at this guy's wound a little and getting under his skin. Probably her intention all along to see what lurked beneath, to see if he had any hidden agendas.

'You two fully acknowledge and accept all this as fact?'

Oh, she's not finished yet. It's Anastassia's and

Jones's turn now.

'I've seen too much to discount the facts,' Jones speaks up.

Good for you, Jones.

'I have had first-hand experience.' Anastassia holds up her fabricated hand.

Was that a little attempt at humour? I can't be sure, but no-one else is smiling. So, I'm not risking the wrath of the terrible two-some over there.

'So, God allowed us to escape? I can tell you, He could've made it easier. Then allowed us to defeat Him, while crossing His fingers and hoping we'd tackle the main problem for Him? Then why wait so long?'

'Possibly because you weren't ready? Possibly as a result of divine arrogance. This is God we're talking about, after all. Maybe it took the last few centuries and His steady decline into madness for Him to finally realise and accept His mistakes. Nobody will ever know for sure.'

Jackson is right: we have to assume the worst. 'So, our next target is a goddess of immeasurable power. Wielding more, in fact, than God himself.'

'Makes sense,' Mist agrees.

I shudder internally. This isn't going to be easy. 'I wish Nyx was here,' I mutter, half to myself.

'Who's Nyx?' Jones asks.

Wow, someone just won't shut up when he gets started. 'You didn't tell them?' I ask Jackson.

'I felt it was need-to-know information, and right now protection of the team was deemed a higher priority than their need to know.'

Okay, I'm liking this guy a little more now, and I also noticed a tiny nod of appreciation from Mist in the periphery of my vision.

'Then when do we begin?'

Mist, straight to the point. And yes, you can bring your axe!

You will need a certain amount of training first regarding weapons usage,' Jackson explains.

Bad move!

'Training! I am no neophyte mortal! I am a warrior, a Valkyrie! I have set foot upon more battlefields than you have had lifetimes!'

Told you so!

Jackson looks a tad uncomfortable now, and Anastassia is gazing at her with a look of wonderment and adoration.

Oh, get a room!

'What I mean is, we should factor in a period with which to bond with the special ops team, and weapons training will be available *if* required. We have to learn to work together as a team and pool our resources, after all.'

'Training!'

She's still a bit miffed.

'I will train your team if they are suited,' she

suggests.

'I don't think that will be necessary. But thank you for the offer.'

And just when things seemed to be going so well.

'Where and when?' I'm getting tired now and want this meeting adjourned, and before Mist flares up again.

'A dormant portal was excavated during the early part of the twentieth century in Saudi Arabia. Its location and purpose have been kept under wraps ever since. And until recently the knowledge required to open it successfully had been lost. The translation inscribed on its surface states that it is essentially only good for one application; then it will lock down, permanently. God, quite possibly, had it installed centuries ago specifically intended for this eventuality.'

'Premeditated?'

'It's just a theory,' explains Jackson.

'So, no way back?' This just gets better. 'And couldn't I just take us all there and back?' I'm confident with my skills to make the suggestion, but something tells me that this isn't going to be a viable option.

Jackson shakes his head.

I knew it.

'Remember, you were allowed a certain freedom of movement last time. That isn't going to be an option this time around.'

'You sure about that?'

He nods.

'Ix?'

He nods again.

'So how do we open it?'

'Ix informed me, it can be done. But I'll reveal the details of that later. But you have my guarantee that it is our only way in.'

Mist snorts in derision and folds her arms.

'Saudi Arabia? Are we going to be safe going in?'

'This is a multinational operation, it's been authorised by the totalitarian monarchy.'

We've been approved, by the king himself! And I'm not talking about Elvis!

'Okay, when?'

'The rest of the ops team are already deployed and awaiting your response and, hopefully, arrival. If the outcome of this meeting was positive, then we were designated to go in a little under two weeks. So that will give you sufficient time to gather your flock. I take it you won't be requiring transport?'

'No, I've got that covered.' Besides, that'll give those military types something to deliberate over when we just magic ourselves out of thin air.

Sophia suddenly springs to mind; she'll probably be touching down in Spain right about now. The special ops boys are just going to love her. This is going to be a real clash of personalities. Hard-nosed soldiers and warrior women, who in a fight would squash those guys flat without even breaking a sweat.

Still, it might be fun. I might even flaunt a little of my own skills just to let them know what I'm capable of. But I'll have to talk to them all first, particularly Maddie. I don't want a petrified platoon supplementing this ancient archaeological site, for the bemusement of wandering nomads and their camels. And, of course, there's Nyx to consider as well, and if you'll excuse my language, she isn't going to take any shit. Perhaps this joint expedition isn't such a good idea after all? But right now, we have no other option, not with only one way in, if Jackson's intel is correct, and I have no reason to doubt him. And already my mind is plagued with too many unquantifiable details, least of all: if we do survive, how do we get home?

'Perhaps we should deal with this ourselves?'

Good for you Mist, just what I was thinking.

'We can take care of ourselves,' Anastassia answers, which seems to satisfy Mist.

Typical!

My turn then. 'I don't doubt that, but my team are ancient beyond your comprehension. They wield powers beyond anything you have yet encountered. I could conjure up a portal right now and cast you into the very depths of the ocean.'

'You could do that?'

At last, a little emotional response from Jones.

'If I wanted to.' Actually, I'm not entirely sure if I could; well, at least not without allowing gallons of icy seawater through. I'm still developing my skills in that field, but he doesn't know that. 'So, why exactly do we need the military again?'

Speechless. Don't blame you, Jones, best keep it shut.

'You need me,' Jackson steps in.

'I've accepted that, but why them?'

'Because they're with me.'

'You're going to have to do far better than that,' Mist responds scornfully, far from impressed.

'Because,' he takes a deep breath, 'what your team tackled previously was nothing in comparison to what will be awaiting us once we cross over. Especially if those creatures we've already previously had experience of are any indication of what's to come. If these things are trying to escape, as Ix suggested, then just what are they attempting to escape from exactly? This situation must be approached with a high degree of caution. And then we have numbers to consider as well. We could well be faced with armies of those things when we arrive.'

Now that conjured up an image that convinced me that any extra help we could muster, would be more than welcome.

'Okay,' I agree, and stare into the pile of scattered images before me. Armies of these things? I hope he's wrong. One image in particular draws my attention. It's like someone grafted a human onto the back of some monstrous beast of elephantine proportions, at least when compared to the vehicle its bulk has crushed beneath it. Its back has been split apart, revealing an unfathomable depth of shark teeth. It is a construct of an insane mind. An army of these, may the goddess help us.

Mist gives her consent with a single nod. Although I get the feeling that she has been waiting and preparing for this moment without exactly knowing what was lurking just beyond the horizon.

'If you allow us until the end of the week to regroup, and we'll update the rest of the team regarding all of this.' I gesture towards the horror show display still adorning my coffee (tea) table.

Jackson nods in acceptance. 'Are you sure you don't require picking up? I could have a chopper here in a couple of hours when you're good to go.'

I shake my head. 'A helicopter,' I explain to Mist. I caught the confusion in her expression: she probably thought Jackson meant an axe when he said chopper. 'No, my way is quicker; it will allow us more time to prepare. All I'll need are co-ordinates.'

'I'll leave Anastassia with you; she has all the details.'

"Nooo!" is what's in my head, but out comes:

'That's fine, I've plenty of room here.' I've already got visions of tree-felling competitions being conducted. Maybe I should mention forming a band now and get them focused on something less destructive?

'Right, well, if we're all done.' Jackson gathers together those horror pics and slots them back into the envelope, before standing up, looking over at Jones, who says nothing. 'Okay, then, so shall we expect you Saturday?'

'Sounds about right,' I confirm. I still intend on us all coalescing out of thin air just to see the expressions on those military faces. Give them all something to ponder over; a little insight into who exactly they'll be amalgamating their forces with.

I don't have anything further to say and so I escort Jackson and Jones — sounds like a cheesy cop buddy movie — as they make their way back to the waiting vehicle.

'Your poor driver. I forgot, I should've offered her something to drink.' I'm genuinely affronted at my lack of social skills.

'It's okay, she had a flask with her,' Jackson answers.

'Is she part of the team?' I whisper, as we approach.

'No, a driver, nothing more.'

They clamber aboard and I stand and watch until the Humvee is far from view and the dust of its departure has dispersed.

That was one hell of a day. I should have gone to Paris with Sophia.

'You okay?'

Mist has joined me as I've been standing here a while.

'Yeah. Didn't see this coming exactly, but I knew this wasn't over.'

'It will be fine,' Anastassia adds. 'We have a good team, only the very best.'

'I hope so, Anastassia, I hope so.'

Well, here goes nothing. 'Hey, have you ever aspired to play the drums?'

'No, but I do play the bass.'

Result!

4

Well then, my silent companion, you've pretty much caught up with events, almost. And it appears that life as you know it is very much under threat; let's be honest, this could be cataclysmic. And knowing that recently departed dear old granny isn't, in fact, reclining on a cloud, strumming on a harp, supping ambrosia, but has been transformed into some monstrous abomination that tears people to shreds, is certainly enough to give the grandchildren nightmares.

It's a bit worrying, isn't it?

I bet you're wishing you'd closed this book a couple of chapters ago? Sorry, too late now — you can't forget that kind of imagery. But perhaps you want to close it now? Pass it on to a friend? Or even better, someone you don't like? Or better yet, donate it to your local Christian charity shop? No? Okay then, let's get back to it.

Let us then skip to the end of the week, the day before we're due to join Jackson and the special ops team. And I'm pleased to inform you that there was no tree felling during that period!

Mist and Anastassia spent a lot of time together

simply walking through the forest; she even left her axe in the house. It's nice that she's finally found someone she feels comfortable enough with to confide in. I have to confess I was a little hurt that she couldn't find it in herself to open up to me, as I've always been here for her. But I'm beginning to think there's a little more than a friendship developing here. I could be wrong, but I'm reading the signs as I see them.

Anyway, let us return to the serious matter at hand. So, where were we?

Well, Maddie and Nyx have returned from New York. I keep active portals in all my properties, as I've mentioned, so it was a swift operation to retrieve everyone. Well, all except Sophia.

Upon my arrival at my New York apartment, I confess I did freak out, greeted as I was by an impressive collection of ornaments and sculptures that had been amassed since I had been there last. I soon realised, after a tentative examination of several of them, that they were just what they appeared to be and not ossified living things. It turns out Maddie has a passion for such collectables and an eye for detail. So it was little wonder that I initially jumped to the wrong conclusion.

I briefed them both on recent events when they returned from the tattoo parlour, and both readily agreed to return with me. Well, what choice did they have under the circumstances? And I got the distinct impression Nyx knew more about the perpetrator and creator of these abominations than she was willing to reveal at present. But I didn't pressurise her, as I was sure she would reveal what she knew when she deemed it necessary. Although, on pondering upon it later, I didn't see how identifying who exactly was behind these blasphemous acts was actually going to aid us in any shape at all.

Maddie posted a quick online update explaining that the tattoo parlour would be closed for the foreseeable future due to a family bereavement. I wish they had just said they were going on holiday; I didn't like the word "bereavement", not under present circumstances at least.

Maddie seemed positively buoyant at the prospect of our forthcoming mission. The mind boggles. I can only assume that the anticipation of ossifying living things without consideration or repercussion was something that appealed to her. An opportunity to let her hair down, so to speak. And while I'm on that subject — no, she doesn't have serpent-hair. At least I've never witnessed such a transformation. She got the idea of gold snakeheads to cap her dreadlocks from the many images of herself that can be readily accessed.

Nyx confided in me later that Maddie had been systematically dispatching much of the lowlife in New York over recent weeks. At the rate Nyx described, she'll soon put the NYPD out of business, and I sincerely hope that they never dredge the Hudson. Of course, the accumulating statues residing on the riverbed did also include Nyx's dinner left-overs as well.

The two of them together make Charles Manson look like a Red Cross volunteer.

Anyway, on to Kal. What a breath of fresh air. Not that I mean anything derogatory towards the others by saying that; she's just so much more relaxing to deal with.

Her defence class regulars were disappointed at her sudden need to depart for a time. I accompanied her to her farewell class, where Kal tried to teach me the mastery of the tuck and roll. But all I could achieve was more of a tuck and slap. I think I've still got a few bruises. But it was touching to see how concerned they all were and they hoped it wasn't anything too serious and that she'd be back soon.

I hope so, too.

That left Sophia. I saw no need in kidnapping her and instead sent her a text:

GOING TO HELL TO DISPATCH DEMONIC GODDESS. ALL HANDS REQUIRED IMMEDIATELY

Granted it was a little OTT, but I needed to get her attention. She arrives back tonight. In fact, she'll be in transit right now. She enjoys flying, by plane I mean — it must come from having wings.

So, we're heading off to Saudi Arabia a little after midnight. They're ahead of us by seven hours, so we'll try to time our arrival and get there first thing in the morning, to a place only referred to as "The Empty Quarter". I wonder why? It doesn't leave anything to the imagination and subsequently doesn't fill me with confidence.

So, I've taken this slight lull in proceedings to hide out in my room and await the impending arrival of Sophia. Leaving strict instructions to leave all the trees and animals alone. Nyx was well fed before we left New York, so no worries on that count at least.

I can still hear the deep *thunk!* of Mist's axe embedding itself in wood. They've taken up axe throwing now! But at least their administrations are solely focused on only one tree. Anastassia is proving to be rather good due to that bionic arm of hers. I actually saw her crush a rock with that hand the other day — very impressive. I pity the individual that gets on the wrong side of her.

So, to recap, you may be thinking Jackson and myself: magical and psychic abilities, very handy. Maddie: a stare that would stop anything living, dead in its tracks. Which did get me thinking: what if everything, where we were going, was dead? I guess we'll find out. Mist and Anastassia: formidable warriors both.

But what of the others?

Sophia, apart from her ability to fly, can wield divine energy and can focus and direct it via her sword. Which I presume will have a devastating effect on all things evil. Now that is going to prove most beneficial. I must confess, I'm rather looking forward to seeing her in action, as her ability had little effect on Him, as He was a divine being Himself. Oh, and I'll get to that little altercation before we relocate to sandier climes.

Now then, we come to the enigma of Nyx, who stood near or at the beginning of Creation and is mother to sleep, death and darkness. If you believe what's written and posted online. Intense, right? So, she's got to know a thing or two. Not that she's very forthcoming with information; but based on her alleged history, she's one I won't be worrying about when we depart.

Apart from her accursed appetite, dispensed by Him, I'm sure she has many hidden talents that will prove valuable to us, as I'm sure even she wouldn't be capable of exsanguinating all our foes single-handedly. There is her shadow form, of course, of which I have personally witnessed. Capable of transforming herself into a smoke-like mist that allows her a certain freedom of movement her physical body would be incapable of. This proves most effective at night. I did wonder if the vampire legend originated from Nyx herself and not Vlad the Impaler at all.

She gave me a few tips on this matter-dispersal property she possesses. I'm not really getting the knack of it, although I can move about at night now almost invisible to anyone if I apply myself and focus. I'll have to try and cajole some further tricks from her in the future.

All in all, then, quite a team.

I didn't forget Kal. Demon slayer and destroyer of evil. I'm confident she will be able to handle anything thrown her way. And finally, the mysterious Ix, our guide through the underworld if nothing else, so quite an indispensable member. Though, apart from that, there were eight cells in that dungeon and one was built for the purpose of detaining her, so she is already a part of the team in my eyes, regardless.

This portal, as well: turns out it's a flat stone disc set in the sand, according to Anastassia — she's been there — the whole surface inscribed with glyphs and symbols and set within a ring of crumbling stone pillars, in the middle of nowhere.

I still don't know how we are to activate it; apparently, only Jackson and Ix are parties to that knowledge. Perhaps I'll get a feel for it when I'm there? Or maybe Jackson will open up a bit more on-site?

Come to think of it, now that I mention Jackson, I'm not fully aware of the extent of his abilities. Sure, he's a powerful telepath; but beyond that, I'm a little in the dark. Even mine seem woefully inadequate to me in light, or rather in dark, of what is surely awaiting us.

Nyx sensed this dilemma within me and

encouraged me to let go of my fears, something Kal has also encouraged me to do over the months; and that our unity as a team was where our real strength lay. I can get with that — perhaps that's why we were segregated for so long? So, I got the impression that our full potential is yet to manifest. Maybe associating with Jackson will unlock talents I didn't even know I had, or he could even teach me a few things like Nyx has been trying to do?

It is at times like these that I console myself with the fact that we have a special ops team to back us up. Although it is one thing tackling insurgents and guerrillas, it is entirely another thing to engage monsters and deities.

That's nice — the laughter, I mean, coming from outside. It's good that they are all taking the time to relax and unwind a little. Who am I to talk? I'm the most wound-up out of all of them! I'll maybe join them in a bit. I can hear the clink of glass, too. I might even partake and indulge in a beer. I don't drink alcohol, but perhaps just one, under the circumstances.

Mist enjoys a beer and despite the amount she can down, she never appears inebriated. I don't know if that's a good or a bad thing. Isn't that the whole point of drinking? To get drunk?

But it is good to have them all back; it can get a bit lonely out here, despite all the amenities I've had installed. The array of solar panels on the roof provides the power and the satellite dish provides the entertainment. But I have, from time to time, moved to New York or London just to experience the noise and the crowds again. But that's the worst kind of loneliness, when you're surrounded by people. And it isn't long before I find myself back here. Give me trees, wilderness and animals any day.

I hope we survive this. It was nice to talk a bit of shop with Jackson; we didn't get much of an opportunity, I know, but it was refreshing. I've never had that kind of freedom regarding my abilities and beliefs before.

He seemed nice, a bit like myself. Tough on the outside, but on the inside… it's just the way you've got to be to survive in this world. But I may just have found a kindred spirit in him.

Kal has her devoted followers. Maddie has Nyx — not a physical relationship as such, they're more like sisters. Sophia has her career and all that entails, and numerous offers of undying love, by all accounts; but then again, those people are sometimes the loneliest. Maybe I should take some time out and try to connect with her more when we get back? Fingers crossed on that score.

Now there's the terrible two-some: Mist and Anastassia, as if I needed to name them. They're like two long-lost siblings reunited. Granted one is blonde and blue-eyed, the other dark with brown-eyes. Still, it's amazing what the right person can do for someone's mental well-being — far better than any prescription drug!

And while I'm on the subject of Anastassia, I can share a little gossip while I've got the time. I'm sure she wouldn't mind.

She was raised in a small rural village somewhere in Russia; I can't remember the name, if I'm being honest. Brought up by her mother and abusive stepdad — seems to come with the territory that, although I know they're not all bad.

Her mother died of cancer when she was still quite young, about eight or nine, I think. Life after that was even grimmer. I shan't go into details as she didn't reveal much during this period in her life, but I think we both have a pretty good idea. She joined the Russian Cadet Corp at sixteen, then the Russian army at eighteen. I wasn't aware that the Russians recruited women at that age. But, apparently, she excelled.

And now, at twenty-eight, she's a corporal in this elite special forces' unit. Formed by recruiting the best each regiment had to offer, a real multi-national affair. She was recruited after losing her arm, her exemplary record singling her out, and the carrot was dangled in the shape of a state-of-the-art prosthetic replacement if she joined this elite force.

Well, there you have it, condensed into a few paragraphs. Still, despite her rather traumatic life, it appears to have fazed her little, and I've got to admit I like her.

Well, before I join them for a beer, or maybe, on reconsideration, a cup of tea might be best. Alcohol clouds the mind and I'll need to be functioning at one hundred percent to open that portal later. Tea it is, then! What a rebel I am!

But you've been patient long enough, reader, wondering about that battle with Him? Okay, fair enough. But don't get too excited; as I've mentioned, the whole event played out a lot easier than I'd anticipated. So, keep your expectations low. Otherwise, it'll be like that time when you'd been so looking forward to the final part of that movie franchise for what seemed like forever, amidst all the advertising and media hype. Then you finally get to see it the day of release and it feels like Christmas Eve. Then it's over and you leave the cinema thinking "was that it?" Okay, just so you know.

Right, where to start.

We'd just left that dungeon and initially arrived back here, Canada, within a magic circle I had up and running especially for the occasion. Set within a circle of birch trees. Ones I told Mist to leave well alone or I said I'd shove that axe so far up her... Anyway, she promised and kept it.

It's so much easier to cast spells outdoors: nature is just so much more conducive when you wish to ensorcell. I've been dying to use that word in the conversation for ages! That's your new word for today, unless you're already aware of it. It essentially means to cast a spell to enthral or bewitch someone or something. It comes from old French — I love the French language. I found out later that Jackson is a natural when it comes to languages; it comes with being so psychic.

Back to the team, and despite their brutal condition, they convinced me to take them with all due haste to accost their tormentor. I couldn't deny them; one for all and all for one, and all that. So, with barely a five-minute respite, we departed once more, this time into battle. Well, almost; you can't go into battle empty-handed, after all.

5

So, a slight detour was called for, and not to some weapons depository here on Earth, but God's own weapons hoard. I'm not talking about some divine DIY superstore either, where everything is stored neatly on shelves or packed away in cases. This was a museum of the celestial, the magical, most potent weaponry you could conceive of.

Whether commissioned by Him personally, constructed by His legions of subordinates, or possibly stolen from defeated foes over the centuries, I couldn't tell you. I just don't know. At the time, I wasn't even entirely sure how we had unerringly arrived here. It later turned out that Nyx had known exactly where we needed to be and had "steered" us here, influencing my magic.

As I was untutored in the handling of weapons, I spent our all too brief time there examining the displayed artefacts like a schoolchild on their first visit to the museum. Sophia, likewise, chose not to indulge; she possessed her sword, after all. Nyx also refrained.

The building was vast and had a pervading atmosphere of neglect and abandonment. We were quite possibly the first visitors this place had received in centuries.

Mist located a battle-axe — no surprises there. Its design was exquisite, the blade filigreed in silver and gold. The wooden handle was elegantly carved, making this piece a work of art in itself. She claims it was fashioned by her people. Although I thought in Nordic myth it was the dwarves that generally forged weapons, I have no reason to doubt her, and my Nordic mythology is rather vague.

Kal selected a fearsome set of swords, six in total, obviously, of various styles and constructed from diverse metals. Some seemed fashioned from minerals I'm quite sure I'd never even seen before.

Maddie picked out a war hammer, its blunt end balanced by an equally-looking fiercely spiked end.

I did reconsider briefly on seeing my team hefting their choices, and I'm quite sure there were many more weapons of a more magical nature hidden amongst the more obvious ones. But much of what I'd viewed was beyond my comprehension; even their very appearance left me completely baffled.

But Nyx did retrieve a small golden orb from one display case. I mean, she actually reached straight through the glass without breaking it, before handing it to me.

'The Star of Ishtar,' she proclaimed mysteriously, without explaining to me how it should be deployed.

I must admit, it wasn't much to look at initially, but the more you studied it, the more you saw. It arrested your attention, resembling as it did some kind of intricate puzzle ball. The interior revealing some kind of prize if you successfully completed a series of convoluted manoeuvres, no doubt. Its surface was interlaced with curved designs and symbols. And I did indeed get the impression that there was something hidden within, something powerful. I could feel it in my palm as it seemed to squirm most disturbingly.

I quickly jammed it in the pocket of my jeans; it was a tight squeeze, but if Nyx was emphatic that I should have it, then she must have a good reason. As it turned out, she was right.

Those who wished weapons were now suitably armed, and we regrouped in preparation for the moment of truth. I was nervous as hell, but when we gathered in a circle and clasped hands, that feeling immediately dissipated as the energy coursed through us all.

Now, after all those centuries of preparation, it was finally time.

6

We didn't require my portal-conjuring abilities or Nyx's influence on this occasion. As we were already located within the celestial realms, it was Sophia that transported us to our next destination, her light wings fully unfurled, and quite mesmerising. As she had been a servant of God in the past, the sword had been presented to her by Him personally; it was this and her own divinity that carried us directly to His sanctuary.

The flaming sword, by the way, is a slight misnomer. Not technically flaming, it is instead suffused with a bright fire-like aura when in her possession, as is Sophia herself when in full Seraph mode. As with most myths and legends, they have a basis in fact, but the details of which tend to bend and distort over time.

I don't recall travelling, I just remember a flash of light, reminiscent of a camera flash. And by the time I'd blinked my vision back into operation, we were there, wherever that was. I still have no idea. The divine realms are infinite, apparently — so quite big, then!

It was a place out with the usual concepts of time and space, that much I gathered. You have to keep an open mind regarding places like this and try not to impose physical constructs from realities you are familiar with; it only obfuscates matters.

So, we had finally arrived in this nowhere place. Inhabited by endlessly swirling mist, or possibly divine aether, from which physical things and living beings are moulded.

This period of hiatus gave us a moment to re-orientate ourselves, and I remained close to Mist. Although the others had noticeably recovered to a degree, she still seemed particularly fragile, and I could sense her pain empathically. I was admittedly very concerned.

'He is here,' Sophia suddenly announced, brandishing her sword, the light it emitted cutting a swathe through the roiling mists.

We all took a stance and focused on the area she had indicated.

At first appearance, the air cleared to reveal a wizened old man, his head slightly bowed, doing absolutely nothing, just waiting.

Looking back now, I'm not sure what I expected; you have so many preconceived ideas of what God should look like: some ancient sage with white flowing beard, garbed in illustrious robes; or something altogether more imposing and formidable. But certainly not this.

Sophia led us onwards, and we fanned out to form

a line. Kal, on our left flank, armed to the teeth, her deep blue skin still largely coated with centuries of dried blood.

I didn't know how my shower was going to cope with all that?

Nyx was next, having chosen her shadow form. Her smoky constitution made her hard to focus on; her contours blurring and trailing behind her as we stalked our prey. Maddie at her side, hefting that lethal-looking hammer. I had misgivings regarding her stony stare, as it was a curse devised by a divinity, so I had to presume they were immune to her look. Perhaps she had drawn the same conclusion? Hence the hammer.

Then, on the right flank, Mist and myself.

I was feeling a bit out of my depth at this juncture: jailbreaking is one thing, but deity eradication is quite another. But I did my best to throw up a defensive shield despite my misgivings, not at all sure if it would prove to be in the least bit effective. All the time being aware of that writhing ball in my pocket.

The old man allowed us to approach without even acknowledging our presence. And I was beginning to think He was just going to allow us to strike Him down. So I was beginning to doubt whether I could personally perform such a task. He was, after all, if appearances were to be believed, an unarmed old man.

My opinion quickly changed, however.

Whether He had waited until we were within

striking distance, or if His natural survival instincts had kicked in, who knows? But the old man blurred and began to grow, gathering the mists about Him like a mini-tornado.

Sophia launched an attack at this point, breaking the spell and inciting the others to follow her lead. Attempting to thwart His transformation, she directed a beam of crackling energy directly into that burgeoning mass. But He merely seemed to just absorb the power and continued to grow.

We spread out and surrounded Him at this point, working in perfect union; a gestalt entity. I threw more energy into that shield spell and it bloomed in intensity as it spread between us, in an effect similar to osmosis. I have to admit I'd never experienced anything like that before — it was exhilarating.

And that is when the battle truly commenced.

That divine mist had been finally completely absorbed and His transformation complete. Into something fifteen to twenty feet tall. Roughly humanoid in configuration, but His shape was in constant flux and was hard to focus on and identify.

A swiftly constructed limb, or a leering lidless eye, formed in the aether, which were all the necessary components He required with which to launch His attacks. His hands congealing into massive gnarled constructs which pummelled the ground, sending shockwaves through our bones. The team leaping to safety time and again to avoid those mighty bludgeons. But we soon regrouped and, gathering our combined resources, we instinctually knew what was required.

Sophia focused that divine energy at those eyes, temporarily blinding Him and confounding His aim. He quickly refashioned eyes in many formats in an attempt to thwart her attack; those of myriad of His creations: reptilian; insectoid; avian. Even what I recognised to be that of a mantis shrimp — a bit obscure that one, but He had all of creation to dip into.

I watched a nature documentary about them once; fascinating creatures, you should check it out if you get the opportunity.

I'm more inclined to believe that it took the combined effort of God and Goddess to create all creatures great and small — it takes two, right? — and He just took the credit. If you believe in the creation myth, of course? Not sure what I believe in right now. But I'm right here battling God! What else can I believe in?

I found I could also focus my skills and bend the beams of light dispensed by Sophia, improving her aim and leaving Him stymied at every turn.

Kal was a blur of arms, like some kind of out-of-control blender. The blades she wielded were a swirl of flashing metal as she constantly chopped, hacked and slashed at those mighty fists that continued to mash and pound.

Maddie had thrown the hammer aside, unable to wield it quickly enough to prove particularly effective, and had pulled her new shades down her nose. Focusing on making eye contact as He began to form multitudes of orbs.

I noticed several of those conjured eyes suddenly losing their colour and going a matt grey, tiny fractures forming around them like wrinkles in flesh, before they were reabsorbed with a puff of stone dust.

Nyx, meanwhile, had stealthily positioned herself aft of Him and was coiling herself for an attack. I could tell by the way her smoky form seemed to contract and condense. Mist was also waiting for the right opportunity, and I instinctually removed the sphere from my pocket in anticipation.

This constant barrage of repelling and attacking seemed to stretch out for hours, but it probably all played out in only a minute or two. Time in these realms is just irrelevant. And consequently, when the killing move was engineered, it was executed swiftly and flawlessly.

Kal, Maddie and Sophia kept His attention focused as Nyx leapt upon Him from the rear and plunged her formless hands deep into the area that housed the numerous eyes, plunging them right up to her elbows.

I didn't expect the bellowing howl of anguish that reverberated through me in response to Nyx's attack. It was something barely recognisable as human. My vision blurred and my head swam as a result. Similar to that feeling the moment before you pass out.

At that precise juncture, His physical form finally solidified into something more human-like; that's all I could say on the matter.

Mist then took her opportunity and rushed forth, my bloody dressing gown billowing in her wake. Leaping into the air, she buried that axe deep in His chest. I'll tell you, for a woman with iron hoops embedded in her flesh, that was quite incredible to behold. Then with a twist, she pulled the axe free and, pushing against His torso with both feet, she flipped over to land in one of those superheroes poses.

That was so cool!

But I did see her wince in pain, the only time I've ever witnessed her succumb to any kind of physical discomfort.

Needless to say, I wasn't standing gawping in admiration at the time — I did that later — instead, without any preconceived idea of what I was intending to achieve, I threw that sphere, which was as eager to go as I was to let it. And with an extra added magical thrust and guidance, sent it straight into that open wound before He reknitted Himself, Maddie managing to solidify the area and encasing the orb to prevent its rejection.

On asking Maddie about this later, she revealed that she had always needed to make eye contact previously for her stare to prove effective. But when working together as we were, she discovered that still through eye contact, she could specifically target certain areas. A new skill, newly discovered. Funny that, directing Sophia's energy beams was kind of new to me, too. I'd never achieved anything quite like that before, either.

Nyx withdrew as soon as the sphere was implanted and we retreated as one.

The result of the deployed sphere was almost instantaneous and monumental.

A split second before it erupted, I noticed a small point of burning light melting flesh and rock alike within the chest cavity of God.

Then came the flash. Fortunately, I had the foresight to cover my eyes sufficiently before it reached its full intensity. This was accompanied by a noise that I can only describe as something similar to a sonic boom. Something you feel more than you actually hear.

I've been to one or two gigs like that.

And that was essentially the end. By the time we had picked ourselves up, the force had sent us all flying; and regathered, slightly mystified at what had just transpired. There was nothing remaining except a few glistening motes that sparkled like glitter as they floated in the air. In retrospect, I should have tried to grab a couple and put them on eBay — genuine god particles! Who am I kidding? Who was going to buy that?

And that was it; no rubble, no lumps of god-flesh,

not even a hair or crater where once He had stood. God was officially dead.

Wow! I never thought I'd ever hear myself say that.

Initially, I found it hard to accept that we had succeeded. Nyx's wry smile kindled a little confidence in our victory, though. But even at this early stage, I still harboured the belief that it had all been just too easy. I mean, this was God, almighty God! It just didn't seem viable.

Like battling one of those ends-of-level bosses on a video game. A few minutes of button pummelling and it was all over.

At the time I didn't know if any of the others harboured their own doubts or suspected that this was only one side of the coin, so to speak. Essentially, taking out the monkey before we tackled the organ grinder. I'm not even religious, or at least I don't subscribe to any one religion in particular, despite recent revelations, but I still felt bad even thinking this way; but essentially that's what it boiled down to.

Looking back now, I suspect Nyx knew, that sardonic smile of hers. But she's hard to interpret at the best of times.

Either way, it had been an auspicious achievement, and now there was nothing left to do but head home. And after murdering a deity, I could certainly murder a cup of tea.

We formed our circle again, Sophia catching my

eye; she needed me to focus this time as we were heading back to the Earth plane. And whether or not the numerous amounts of practice I'd had conjuring recently? Whether it was our connection? Or just whether it was because I really wanted a cup of tea? We arrived almost instantaneously (I suspect it might have been a combination of all three).

My cup of tea had to be delayed and I had to make do with one of those awful ones dispensed from a vending machine at the hospital, as Mist became my next immediate priority.

I quickly ushered the others into my home and showed them where the food was stored and turned the tap on and off, displaying this feature of modern life so that they could at least deal with their most basic needs. If goddesses even required that kind of sustenance? I didn't even consider that at the time. Then I quickly transported Mist so she could receive immediate medical attention.

It took me a few attempts to open up a portal in the hospital car park, safe enough for us to cross without being witnessed or raising too many questions concerning our sudden arrival. And half-carrying her, barely conscious as she was by now, around to the main entrance and straight to A&E, where I was quickly relieved of my burden. And well, you know the rest of this story. And yes, I did manage to prise that axe out of her hand and give it to Kal for safekeeping before we departed.

So, you're pretty much up-to-date with events now. I mean, there are small details regarding the team's overall recovery over the following months and integrating themselves into this brand-new world. But they adapted surprisingly quickly, an ability I attributed to their divinity. But as I mentioned before, sometimes it's the simplest of things that obfuscate them. Like Nyx and my microwave, and it's not even a particularly complicated one. But she can navigate the internet like a seasoned pro. And Kal struggles with mobile phones. I don't know what it is exactly. I mean, she has learned to use one for business purposes mainly and so we can keep in touch, but she hasn't taken to them with the ease of other more complicated twenty-first-century gadgets.

Mist has found it the hardest to adapt and I think that's understandable under the circumstances. She just refuses to leave this wilderness environment and venture forth; it just doesn't interest her.

But there have been many more light-hearted moments along the way. Nyx's fascination for digital music being one. Her wonder at my iPod and the thousands of songs it stores never ceases to amaze her. And Maddie's love of my old pick-up. Well, she's not that old really, but she's clocked up a few miles now. Turns out Maddie's quite the mechanic. She got that old girl running better than I can ever remember. And don't even get me started on Sophia's initial fascination with my ultra-HD television — talk about square-eyes!

So there have been many highs and lows, as you would expect. But after a few weeks of convalescence and the return of Mist into our family, things improved, and it was a few weeks after that when they began to disperse and seek a little space from each other.

It wasn't anything negative, nobody fell out with anyone. But if you've ever lived in an all-female environment for any period, then you probably know what I'm referring to. And remember, these were essentially goddesses, so the atmosphere was intense a lot of the time — all that ancient transcendent energy flying around!

Besides, I got the feeling that they simply wanted to explore this new world; after having witnessed much of it via the television, they wanted to experience it for themselves first-hand. I can't say I blamed them; after all, they had all been incarcerated for centuries, and now, at last, they were free to roam.

7

Back to the present; and the rest of the evening, as we awaited the arrival of Sophia, was good. It was one of those nights filled with light and laughter. Good company, good tunes and a good cup of tea — for me at least.

I took the opportunity to play a few classic rock tracks as well, and hopefully inspire some desire to form a band amongst those gathered.

I'm planting seeds; I think it's a cool idea anyway.

Maddie, Mist and Nyx cleared out the house of beer. I only bought it in for guests (like I get visitors!), but they made short work of it. Turns out Anastassia doesn't drink. I think that comes as a result of having a boozy step-dad.

I can't ever recall Sophia partaking, and Kal is too mind- and body-conscious to indulge. At least I've got someone to drink tea with. Anastassia's sticking to water, says it's so good out here. And it is, filtered straight in from the lake nearby.

The evening was fragrantly warm, the sunset beautiful and even the mosquitoes had finally met their match in the form of Maddie, as she demonstrated her developing skills, which proved highly effective on these tiny irritating organisms. She can ossify as many of these creatures as she wants, and if I ever go camping, she's coming with me; better than any citronella repellent.

By the time Sophia arrived, my head was reeling with tales about feuding deities, tales from the battlefield, magical conflicts and of realms I'd believed belonged only in the pages of fiction. I tell you, if I could get all this down on paper? But it would take several years and several volumes to do it all justice.

Some of the details discussed jolted loose memories deep in my subconscious, others I recalled from reading numerous volumes over the decades. And not restricted to works of non-fiction either. It turns out that there's a multitude of facts hidden away in the guise of fiction as well. I knew it! I'd always suspected as much.

Well, all in all, it was a night that I'll always remember and cherish for many years to come. Sophia regaled us with stories concerning famous names and faces and the details regarding her recent fashion tour, now cut short. But I shall reframe from naming names; some people just have no shame!

But inevitably the conversation veered towards more serious matters regarding our forthcoming jaunt to hell, as we filled Sophia in on the details.

Well, not hell as you would imagine it. This world,

Earth, is teeming with evil in many guises: people; industry; the usual suspects. We experience it and interact with it every day of our lives, whether we choose to recognise it or not. Well, if you can imagine that but with the dial turned up to eleven, that's about the best way I can describe it. But to be honest, I'm still pretty much in the dark about what exactly we're going to encounter down there. I say down there, but that isn't technically correct either; it's more like taking a side step into a different reality.

I'm far from looking forward to it; I would be an idiot if I was, and I'm not that. I'll certainly be wearing my big ass-kicking boots for this trek. And to reach our target we have to navigate a lovely little place called purgatory — home to the newly dead — sounds like a show on Fox. But hopefully Jackson's friend, Ix, will guide us safely through. But if I'm honest, I'm not entirely convinced I'll be returning from this sojourn. The odds just seem insurmountable.

It's just gone midnight and it's time we prepared ourselves; we've prevaricated long enough. It'll be about 7am in Saudi Arabia right now. I do not expect many tourist attractions in "The Empty Quarter", or facilities either. My little facetious distractions you'll find will become more frequent from here on in; it's a sign of nerves, so you'll have to indulge me. A defensive reaction when confronted with all things evil, and demonic. Pretty much anything that wants to rip my head off and suck the meat off my bones — KFAlice!

The three bathrooms were busy for the next hour as we made the most of hot running water and fluffy towels. I don't think there's going to be much of those available in the desert.

We'd eaten earlier, or as much as I could force down and safely keep down. Nyx had "dined", and apart from Anastassia, the others could subsist on next to nothing. I'm pretty sure that they only eat out of curiosity half the time.

Then we all dressed accordingly for the mission ahead. Sophia was a bit reluctant to change out of her designer cocktail dress, which was absolutely to die for, but practicality triumphed in the end.

Mist and I went for the all-leather look; not the best choice with regards to wet and cold conditions, but durable. Kal, in her army surplus combat gear. Don't know how that's going to work out when she's got six arms on the go? (Turns out that's how she arrives in Saudi; she'd already custom-altered the garment to accommodate her extra limbs.)

Sophia looked knock-out in black thigh-length boots, roll-top sweater and knee-length leather coat. Maybe not the most pertinent of choices, but what do I know? I've never been to hell; for all I know, all the newly dead are all wearing roll-top sweaters? What a fool I'd look then!

Maddie's developed a Goth-look and Nyx, via her

shadow form (don't know exactly how she manages this), can shift and re-form to wear any item of clothing she desires. And on this occasion had opted for mimicking Anastassia's military garb.

You know the age-old question: "If you had a superpower, what would it be?" And more often than not people say "invisibility" — yawn, boring! No imagination, most people. Well, I'd have Nyx's ability to fashion any item of clothing I so desired — how cool is that? Wear all the latest designer gear at no expense. I even noticed Sophia giving her a look of admiration; I think there was even a note of envy in there as well.

It was time.

Kal retrieved her holdall containing her array of swords and Mist has her axe — she even bought a holster for it online. She was like a kid impatiently waiting for Christmas until it finally arrived. Delivery can take a while out here in the sticks. Guns, if we required any, would be supplied upon arrival. Although I feel far more confident relying on my natural abilities. I've watched plenty of zombie flicks, though, and a headshot seems to work every time. So I may reconsider before we descend to those dark realms. I'm just keeping my options open.

Back in the birch circle again. House is secured and tidied to my specifications. I hate coming back to housework and a sink full of dishes. Kal's great at dishes; she can wash, dry and stack all at the same time!

Anastassia provided a map of the area we'd be travelling to. I say a map — it's just nothing with an "x" and some co-ordinates. I've never travelled purely relying on longitude and latitude before, so I hope we don't end up miles from anywhere.

Oh, hang on, that's exactly where we're going!

We link hands and that current flows through us like static and all my doubts and misgivings evaporate; just those regarding our safe arrival at least — I've still plenty more concerning the trip after that.

Suddenly, the scent of somewhere exotic and foreign fills my nostrils. Warm and dry but somehow fragrant, like the faintest trace of incense lingering in the air. The way was open.

See you on the other side of the world.

8

Oppressive heat and sand as far as the eye could see assailed us as we made our rather ostentatious arrival. That and the presence of a small military camp, of course. Bringing all those present to a wide-eyed standstill and silencing conversations.

Anastassia sort of spoiled the moment just then by throwing up. It was her first experience of travelling by this method, and to be fair it can be rather disorienting.

Just to clarify: generally, when I portal cast it is very much like opening a door which I can simply step through, unless utilising my birch circle, in which case it more resembles teleporting. But being in physical contact with the rest of the team certainly boosts my capabilities and I'm able to essentially "beam" us directly to our required destination.

Sophia, like Kal, had arrived in her unsullied condition, as before our decampment it was decided that there would be no need for deceptions here. Our true identities would be revealed soon enough, so we saw no need to shroud ourselves; therefore, I had disentangled my perception filter cloaking Kal.

I suppressed a smile as several in attendance took a

few steps back in awe, but mainly out of reverence for Sophia, and fear regarding Kal — all blue, many-limbed and angry-looking. She always looks angry when in that form, doubtless to inject terror into her demonic prey. Although they had all been previously briefed on our imminent arrival, the reality still came as something of a shock to them.

Jackson and Sergeant Jones — who bellowed orders for the gathered troops to continue with their duties — hurried forward to greet us. An older guy was in their wake, who I took an immediate dislike to. The hard look in those grey eyes and confident stride told me that he was in command of this operation. Or, to be more precise, in command of the troops within his platoon. Myself and my crew were under no obligations to bow to military jurisdiction here — so let him try.

I smile at Jackson; it's only been a few days, but I've missed him — hardly know him really, but still, I feel we have a connection. He returns the smile, flashing those white teeth. But he looks tired, the bags under his eyes are a new addition since we last interacted.

'Jones, good to see you again.' I dispense with his military rank; I've not got much time for authority. Besides, as far as I was concerned, we were in charge here and I'm quite sure my crew would back me up in that assumption. These uniforms couldn't even begin to comprehend what they'd signed up for here; in a way I pitied them. For some of them at least, this desert was the last time they were going to set foot in this realm ever again.

'Alice,' he nodded curtly. Before acknowledging the rest of the team, who had formed a line to my left. 'Let me show you around and introduce you all.'

Straight to business. Although I don't know what he was going to show us that we couldn't already see from our vantage point. But he remained very professional in light of who had just arrived in camp and was doing a fine job not staring, particularly at Sophia, who was still attracting a lot of attention. Even Jackson was quite mesmerised until I elbowed him.

I'll let him off; you'd stare too if you'd seen her.

Anyway, the temporary camp consisted of five tents the colour of sand; two reserved for sleeping quarters — one male and one female. Including Anastassia, there were four female recruits in attendance. A mess tent, and a medical tent. The latrine was situated a short distance away, for obvious reasons, as despite the chemicals used, the smell was still impossible to mask in this heat. And finally, the equipment repository.

The tour was over before it had barely begun. The black-clad troops eyeing us uncertainly the whole time through their designer shades.

Black! In this heat? Talk about masochistic! And dammit! Forgot my own sunglasses; I'll have to try and appropriate a pair while I'm here.

Then we were led to where the portal was located. I spotted the circle of stone pillars, little more than stumps really — the sand-laden winds had abraded them to mis-shapen stumps a few feet in height, a short distance from camp.

'You ready for this?' Jackson asked, as we trudged through the shifting sand.

I'm sure I can feel grains in my boots already. How did that happen? I raise an eyebrow. 'Not really, but what choice do we have?'

He nods. I can see the strain on his face, and he falls silent once more. In fact, the whole atmosphere in this place is very oppressive, and I can feel it pressing down on us as we reach the site.

Tillson's caught up with us now; he hasn't even introduced himself yet, him of the steely eyes. I find out later he's a general. After he had well and truly scrutinised us, he had detoured into one of the tents, to radio in our arrival to his superiors, no doubt, before catching up with us at the ruins. I don't like him; he comes across as a man with hidden agendas. Nyx flashes him a toothy grin and he takes a step back and also gives Kal as wide a berth as possible without losing face. He's already lost face in my eyes. If they were running a sweepstake on who gets monster-chewed first, then my money's on him.

'I'll take it from here, Jones.'

'Very good, sir.' Jones salutes and beats a hasty

retreat. Despite his stoicism, I reckon he was still a bit distressed at some of my team's appearance. His hasty retreat is rather hampered by the sand, and I try not to laugh as he stumbles off.

'Alice?' Tillson asks, fishing for a surname.

'Just Alice will do.' I'm not making things easy for him and I'm not here to make friends. So, if he wants a battle of wills, then he's already lost. I don't go in much for that alpha-male bullshit.

'Okay, Alice, and…?'

I introduce everyone as if he doesn't know who we are already, but social etiquette and all that.

He nods. I can feel it coming.

'Well, Alice, my name's General Tillson and just so you're aware, I'm in charge of this operation…'

And there you have it; didn't take him long.

'Tillson,' Maddie steps up. 'Perhaps in your minuscule world you believe you govern here, maybe your men even believe that.' She gestures towards the camp with an arm. 'But in reality, we have natural supremacy over you mortals, so you would be well advised to pay heed to our guidance.' She folds her arms across her chest defiantly. 'If you wish to continue living, that is.'

'Was that a threat?'

Tillson's gone a bit red and I don't think it's because of the sun.

'Yes.' Nyx smiles at him, but it's not friendly.

Jackson throws his hand up. 'General, perhaps you should focus on your troops. I'll take care of Alice and her team. What do you say?'

Tillson attempts to stare down Jackson, but he's not backing down. Using some of that Jedi mind stuff on him, I hope.

After a few seconds, the general relents.

'Very well. But this is a military operation and in my eyes these people are civilians. Just keep them under control, understand?'

And he marches off. Typical: he had to get the last word in. I give Maddie a little shake of my head as I can see her preparing to accost him further. Better leave well alone, I think. We won that first round; best not to antagonise things any further.

'Well, that went well.'

I can't tell if Mist is being sarcastic or not.

'Bloody military.' Jackson shakes his head and leads us through the stone ring onto the stone disc itself. 'But they've been sitting on this site for the last six months. I only became aware of it eight weeks ago. They're more informed than I'd anticipated. A necessary evil at the moment, I'm afraid.' He addresses the whole team. He's obviously not happy about their presence either.

'Don't worry about it, we can work with this,' I assure him. I hope so anyway; otherwise, we might be leaving a stone platoon in our wake.

'Are they all aware of what lies ahead?' Kal asks, examining the engravings on the surface of the stone.

'Most, yes, have had direct contact with those... incursions.'

'These markings are very ancient,' Kal remarks.

'The first language,' Nyx adds.

Kal nods in agreement. 'This is a blood sigil.' She stands up, her examination complete.

I know exactly what she means. It will take the spilling of blood to open this doorway.

'I vote Tillson,' Mist offers. She is slowly pacing the perimeter of the stone disc, which is about twenty feet in diameter and has been recently cleared of sand. Without that kind of constant attention, it would be swallowed up in only a few days and lost forever. 'I will sacrifice him if you so require.'

It's not even a question, just a statement of fact.

'I don't think that's going to be necessary.' I'm quick to step in. 'Is it?' I turn to Jackson; this is his area of expertise, I hope.

'Only blood spilt by a willing sacrifice will open this portal,' Kal confirms, staring at Jackson as if challenging him to contradict her.

'Is she right?' I know she is.

'It's the only way.'

'Who?'

'We don't know yet.' He stares across at the camp.

So, it's one of them. Well, it couldn't be one us,

obviously. And although I'm no stranger to spilling my own, I don't think my body contains enough blood to sufficiently fill those inscriptions. 'Do they know?'

He shakes his head.

'Only when the moment is upon us will their identity be revealed. The energies are still in flux at this stage, the one to sacrifice themselves still undecided.'

Thanks, Sophia, despite the heat I've got goose bumps. Is it me or has the temperature just dropped?

'This is dark, powerful magic,' Nyx adds. 'Their weakest link will succumb in time. Until then we must be patient.'

And with that, she heads for camp, Mist and Maddie following in her footsteps.

What? That's it? 'Haven't you got a camel or a goat or something?' I feel bad for asking, but we're talking human sacrifice here.

'The blood must be human,' Kal verifies.

And my feet are freezing now.

Jackson notices my discomfort as I shift my feet. 'It's quite a sensation, isn't it?'

'You can say that again. Any idea what's underneath?'

'Sand.'

Huh! I should've guessed that: it's a portal, not an elevator.

'We should re-join the others?' Sophia says.

Kal has already left and Sophia urges us on. 'The

darkness here will attempt to discompose your thoughts and manipulate outcomes. We would do well to avoid this ruin until the portal has been opened. Come.'

She leads myself and Jackson back to camp. And who are we to refuse the offer of a Seraph?

In case you're curious, and I'm sure you are, when in her angelic form she appears the same, but her aura is in full effect. Infused with this golden light that seems to radiate out of her and forms three pairs of "wings" that flutter and pulse. That's the best way to describe it; the whole effect is quite spellbinding. Once you begin to stare, it's hard to pull your attention away, and then she's got that whole floating hair thing going on, like she's submerged underwater. But since she had it cut short, the effect isn't quite as distracting.

I had noted as well that although the rest of us walked upon the stone circle, Sophia hovered just above it, never setting foot on the surface. Oh, she goes barefoot in this form as well. I think it's that humility thing again — old habits! Whereas she does normally make contact with the ground when walking, or it's more like a glide really. Either way, her avoidance in making direct contact with the stone spoke volumes in itself.

Now that we had exited the circle, she had returned to earth and my feet were already sweating with the heat.

'So, how long do we have to wait?'

'Until the sacrifice has been chosen? Not long.'

'How can you be so sure?'

Jackson scratches his head before answering, and I'm not surprised he's itching, wearing a woollen hat out here.

'Ix informed me.' He rolls his eyes up at the hat jammed on his head. 'It keeps the volume turned down; you know, muffles things a bit.'

I instantly know what he's referring to. Psychic emanations and transmissions. I get a bit of that myself, but I've never felt the need to wear a hat or a tinfoil crash helmet. I've never been much of a hat person anyway.

'Has she been in touch?' I ask, referring to Ix.

'If and when she can. The dreams since I've been here have been pretty intense.'

I don't question him any further about this. Dreams can be very diverse and a dispensary of knowledge and prophecy if you know how to interpret them properly once proficient in their navigation. Instead, I try to lighten the mood, indicating his headwear.

'You tried tinfoil?'

'Doesn't work, it amplifies.'

Wow, he's serious, he's actually tried it; it must get bad in there.

'So, we just wait, then?' We've reached camp.

'We just wait,' he replies.

The others await us on the periphery of the

encampment and Nyx catches my troubled expression.

'One life sacrificed to save potentially thousands, probably millions. It is justifiable.'

I know she's right; I'm just very uncomfortable with the idea — but that could be the influence this place is having on me as well.

'So, do you want me to show you to your bunks? Or do you want to learn how to handle a gun?'

Well, no way could I lie on my bunk now, my head turning this latest development over and over. Perhaps firing off a few rounds will make me feel better. 'You armed?' I'm curious to know how far his dislike of guns has stretched.

He lifts one side of his jacket to reveal a holstered pistol. 'I'm not taking any chances.'

Point taken. 'Okay, perhaps you'd better show us what's on offer.'

He leads us over to the weapons repository. The rest of my crew in tow. Nobody's even attempted socialising or mixing with the soldiers yet, and the already tense atmosphere is even more strained now.

'You trust me, don't you?' Jackson asks me, as he holds back the tent flap and secures it in place.

'Yes, I trust you,' I reply. At least more than the military squad.

He smiles gratefully. 'Thank you.'

And he means it. This is the first time I've met someone as enhanced as he is. Okay, I've passed people in the street or spotted someone in a restaurant who stood out from the crowd, but not like this. Still, he is one of the eight, the original crew. I wonder who he once was? Merlin, maybe? Or was he a fictional creation? Mind you, that doesn't mean anything; maybe, like myself, he simply doesn't remember. But one thing's for sure: he's lonely; that's something I'm picking up on loud and clear.

'You sure you've not got that thing foil-lined?' I give him another friendly dig. I want to see that smile again. And there it is.

'Believe me, I've tried everything, but natural fibres seem to work the best.'

I nod. That makes sense.

'But the living haunt me, you know?' He lowers his voice as the others fill the interior of the tent while I remain beside him.

I nod. I think I do know.

'Small groups I can handle. You and your team, no problems; but that lot.' He nods over at the troops milling about. 'It's like having people over at your house and they have no respect; you know, leave it in a mess: cigarette butts in the carpet; spilt drink; scratched vinyl.'

Scratched vinyl! Sacrilege. 'Houseguests from hell,' I laugh.

'But in here' — he taps his head — 'there are one or two exceptions. Anastassia's one, Big K's all right as well, but the majority…' He tails off.

'I take it Big K's the bear in the uniform?' He's hard to miss.

'Kosovan, hence the K. But he's a real gentle giant, considerate — most of the time — when he's not showing off in front of his mates anyway.'

That's one thing about the military mind: their child-like simplicity when it comes to nicknames. It's probably so they can remember everyone's name.

There's a black South African in camp. X, they call him, as in Malcolm X. A bit racist, I thought initially, but he's a fan of the human rights activist and consequently quite happy with his tag.

Then there's Hotdog, originally from Memphis, Tennessee. Holds the record in his platoon for eating the most hotdogs in one minute — twenty-one! Time must just fly by here in camp!

Mel, actually Deek, but it's Mel here, who hails from Scotland. Mel Gibson played William Wallace in *Braveheart*. You get the picture? The list goes on. You'll meet more of them shortly.

But for now, look at all this hardware. I can already see Kal has her eye on that fifty calibre. I've played a bit of Xbox in my time; I'm not too shabby with my weapon ID.

'It's good you're here, though; you know, someone I can relate to, because this place is so… unhealthy.'

Wow, Jackson is really shook up; this place has

affected him deeply. He sees the inquiring look in my eye.

'Wait until you've been here a few days, you'll see what I mean.'

He wasn't exaggerating.

9

I'm going to jump ahead a bit here. There are only so many times you can talk about sand getting into everything.

So, we're five days in and the tension is building. Everyone can feel it now, even the thickest of those military skulls. Something's going to give, and soon.

I've had to up my psychic shields and the others have become more introverted; nobody's speaking much and we're just going through the motions at the moment. Even Sophia's radiance seems a little duller than usual.

Jackson appears to be affected the most and I've helped him as much as I can by channelling energy his way and constructing a shield around him. It seems to help and we let him bunk in with us girls. Which eased his burden a little; maybe he should try one of those deep-sea diver's helmets?

But the nightmares he suffers. He won't relate the details, but you can see it in his eyes — haunted.

The rest of the crew don't mind his presence; he is one of us, after all. We also have the company of Anastassia, Chow, Sanchez and Sam. The women's blatant disregard for their semi-nakedness at times rather embarrasses him, and he quickly finds something else with which to occupy his mind; it's quite sweet really. At least he respects us, unlike some of those other idiots in camp.

But we've reached a kind of parity, or at least we let them believe that. We know who's really in charge here. But trust me, there were several sabre-rattling moments over the last few days. I'll take a moment to relate my favourite instances as I lie on my bunk in an attempt to escape that relentless heat. It's the number one pastime around here. At least when Tillson gives the recruits a break. I got sick of the sound of his voice on day one. I know it's wrong, but if there's going to be a sacrifice...

I must admit, the others are coping far better than me in these conditions; but considering their previous internment, I suppose it comes as not much of a surprise.

Firstly, and I have to admit I was waiting on this one from the moment we arrived, one of the platoon members finally made a lewd remark directed towards Sophia. They managed to reel it in until day two.

Sophia swept up to him — that was the only way to describe the rapid movement — and caught him by the legs. Cobra was his name, London born, a snake tattoo encircling his bicep. Well, the next thing, she disappears into the blue, trailing him upside down in her wake. Everybody in camp went quiet; even the few bodies sheltering in the tents came out to watch.

It was several minutes before they returned. I was quite relieved, because I did consider the possibility that she was going to dump him miles from camp, possibly from a great height.

The guy was obviously distraught; no sympathy for him, though, and he had soiled himself. Now they call him Pampers, and he keeps his mouth shut.

That's one to us.

Maddie planned her demonstration in advance, collecting a meagre collection of wildlife over three days: three leggy beetles, a scorpion and a rather bemused-looking lizard. There's not much life out here, except us. She then gathered the platoon around and did the deed on those poor animals; not the platoon, I hasten to add. Which received one or two whoops. Nice demo; they don't bother her.

Two up.

Kal didn't have any problems at all; she generally gets on with everyone. I think they want to adopt her as their mascot.

Nyx? Well, I've seen quite a different side to her since our time out here. She has many facets and is very complicated, I reckon it's an age thing, although she doesn't look a day over thirty. That applies to them all; ancient though they are, they have maintained their youthful looks, purely out of vanity, I presume. Wouldn't you?

Her sense of humour is so dark it seems to bypass most. I get it, but I've known her a while. Her jokes are delivered with a toothy smile and a glow of those golden irises. She freaks them out a bit. I've been hanging out a lot with her since we've been here.

So, that's three-nil. Four, if you're counting Kal's congeniality.

Mist was another that attracted a lot of unwanted attention. Not possessing any powers as such that could be demonstrated, she simply picked out the two hardest-looking recruits: Big K and a guy called Thumper — Belgian, I think. And challenged them to a fight, bare-knuckle.

They readily, and stupidly, agreed.

Well, what a disappointment! Five seconds later, two fewer teeth, a split lip and a minor concussion and it was all over. And she wasn't even trying. Anastassia enjoyed the show immensely and said something derogatory to the two of them where they were sat recovering in the sand. It was in Russian, but I'm pretty sure it was the kind of thing I'd be uncomfortable translating.

'I should have picked four of you and at least made it challenging,' Mist remarked, before stalking off.

Game well and truly over.

Tillson stepped in at that point and called a halt to proceedings, scared we were going to break his soldiers. I think Mist was beginning to enjoy herself. No trees to cut down here, just soldiers.

So that left me. I could see it coming; they had no-one left to target. It was time for me to draw the proverbial line in the sand. And it was a guy called Sweets who finally lit the fuse. Funny how the women refrained from winding us up; female intuition, they knew better.

Sweets, so-called because he always had a pocketful of hard-boiled sweets, to match his hard-boiled head!

'So, pixie-girl, what's your superpower? Looking hot?' The laughter from his friends was rather forced and I noticed one or two sauntering off.

That's the best he could think of after almost four days? Now you know what we're dealing with here.

I was a tiny bit flattered that he thought I was hot, but more annoyed that he'd slighted my height by referring to me as a pixie. Hey, I'm five foot six! Besides, I had my team to consider, and I was aware of some of them looking over in interest, awaiting my riposte.

So, I sauntered over to him, a stupid grin on his face. Hadn't they learned over the last few days? Maybe they'd drawn lots to see who got to antagonise who?

I quickly opened up a portal directly behind him and with a little mental shove — I think I have Jackson to thank for helping me a little there, as my telekinesis has never been the best — through he went. Portal sealed — job done!

The exit was only just over some dunes that bordered our camp and a few feet in the air. I'm getting good at these; I must confess I gave an inward sigh of relief when he stumbled back into camp twenty minutes later, looking hot and bothered, to the sounds of jeers and laughter.

But once complete, our time here relaxed a bit. It was a rites-of-passage in a sense; all the recruits went through it, and we were no exception. And I think it alleviated the boredom. We still pretty much kept ourselves to ourselves. Mist hung out with Anastassia and Mel, who'd known Anastassia for a couple of years and were "tight", as they would say. And Jones seemed to be attached to Tillson by an invisible leash. But the general kept his distance, probably scared of what we'd do to him, because his rank certainly wasn't going to grant him immunity.

I asked Jackson when I got the chance whether he had had to undergo this "ceremony" when he'd arrived.

On his first day, apparently, he was on his own after all. He was pulled up by Tillson in front of the whole squad, and barked at like some wet-nosed recruit. Well, Jackson whipped his hat off — said it muffled out-going transmissions as well — and gave him a mental jab, just a little one.

Tillson regained consciousness five minutes later, with a headache and a bloody nose.

Hah! Totally awesome; no wonder he tends to avoid us.

Jackson reckons he could've taken his head off if he'd really put his mind to it; you know, like in that film *Scanners*? His words. I've never seen it; I'll have to check it out some time. He's growing on me more and more — Jackson, not Tillson; even Maddie and Nyx chat away to him, and that isn't like them. I guess they recognise a kindred spirit in him, same as me.

I've noticed as well my powers have been turned up a notch. I don't know whether it's this place or that seven out of the eight have been reunited. It makes me wonder what things will be like when Ix finally joins the ranks.

We also spent a day weapons training, which was fun. Sophia absconded for a while to stretch her wings, literally; her sword is the only tool she would require. But the rest of us took part, even Nyx, which surprised me. I think she just didn't want to be left out.

This took place on day two. Some of us had already picked out a few choice bits and pieces from the armoury the day before and we took out our frustrations on the circle of stone pillars, what was left of them anyway, and there's even less left of them now.

I stuck to something lightweight and manageable, a pair of Walther PPKs; I remembered Bond uses those. Not sure if that was the best reason for my choice, but I kind of like them in the holsters I have strapped to each leg — very Lara Croft.

Maddie and Nyx went for AK-12s, I think they were — assault rifles.

'Russian, good choice,' Anastassia commented on seeing what they had chosen.

I was surprised Mist didn't rush off and swap her Uzi for one after hearing that. I didn't even know they still used Uzis, but Mist claimed she preferred the compact size.

And Kal did claim that fifty-calibre machine gun; don't ask me what kind it was, but it was big and heavy — I could barely lift it. She still retained her swords, held in a custom-made scabbard strapped to her back. Which held four of the swords she had relinquished from that divine armoury: two demon-slaying blades, black and sinister-looking, forged especially for purpose: the dispatching of demons; two Japanese samurai swords, which she said she bought from a contact she had met through her defence classes; a total pirate cutlass, which she claims belonged to Anne Bonny, a famous Irish pirate? I can't say I've heard of her, and how did her sword end up in God's armoury anyway? Presumably, He had very eclectic tastes. And a short stabbing sword called a Xiphos; she says it's Greek and very old. And to finish her look, a string of incendiary grenades fashioned into a necklace for her by the guys in the crew — how thoughtful.

But looking back, it was a fun day and I discovered

I'm a terrible shot. Mist isn't much better either: her shots go as wide as mine. And I suspect Jackson has spent many an hour gaming, because he's really good. And Kal, it just comes naturally to her; defence, offence, she's got it covered.

But as this, our fifth day, draws to a close, reality is creeping in like winter frost. The nights are getting noticeably cooler, and that's not because of the weather.

Supplies have been doled out: ammo; water canteens; food supplements; headsets with comms units; tiny cameras and flip-down night sights attached. I am so stealing a pair of those.

The troops are carrying extra rations and further ordinance, and I haven't a clue what most of it is. Me, I'm going light: my two guns, spare clips and water canteen. I don't plan on being down there that long.

Out of the thirteen — ominous number that; seems a bit too coincidental to me now that I think about it — only nine will be accompanying us. The remaining four are tasked with packing up camp for immediate evacuation once we're on our way. Or, to be more precise, three will be doing the packing, which by then will include one body.

So, with us are Tillson (boo!); Anastassia; X; Big K; Pampers; Thumper; Sanchez; Mel and Chow, who, for the first half day, I thought was a guy, until she bunked in with us; she's butch. Chinese, as her tag would suggest, but it's actually because she can eat! A lot! Sanchez doubles as the cook, and that's her actual name; maybe they figured if they annoyed her too much, she'd do stuff to their food. Of Latin American descent; I haven't spoken to her much, but she seems nice, does an amazing veggie curry. Who knew that the military catered for Veggies? Can't say it's something I'd ever thought about before.

So, that means Jones won't be coming along; shame, I quite like his quiet ways. I did ask Jackson if we could swap him for Tillson, but he just laughed. That was a no, then.

Not much of a squad to accompany us really; I'd half expected a small army. Jackson must've guessed what I was thinking, or more likely heard my thoughts, because I picked up his response loud and clear in my mind: "expendable numbers". Great, so these troops weren't expected to return.

So, what about the rest of us?

Hotdog, Sweets and Sam — an Iraqi woman. They call her Sam because they can't pronounce her name, but the first three letters are S-A-M. I think she's possibly there as we're close to Iraq, keeping an eye on things. I don't know how relations are between Iraq and Saudi. I tend to avoid such political and military feuds and pacts; it's hard to keep up with, and if I'm honest it doesn't particularly interest me. So those are the lucky ones who won't be joining us.

So, there you have it: we're pretty much good to go,

we're just waiting for the inevitable, and I'm not ashamed to admit it, but I'm scared and I can't help worrying about who it's going to be. As it turned out, we didn't have to wait much longer to find out. It was 3am the following morning.

I was woken by a commotion outside and I knew immediately what was behind it. The air was frigid and I could see my breath misting before me.

The portal was open.

The tent was emptying fast as I clambered into my chilled clothes and snapped the buckles tight on my boots — after shaking them out in case of scorpions; that's a thing here.

Nyx remained while the others left to regroup on the platform. 'It was Jones.' She laid a hand on my shoulder in consolation. 'Once they had arrived, the outcome was inexorable. Our presence here could not have prevented or deferred the outcome.'

I know she speaks the truth. But not Jones. I liked him, he was so complaisant.

She left me then in a flurry of darkness as I strapped on my two holsters.

This was it!

Pre-dawn had painted a streak of deep purple on the horizon, which in any other circumstances would be considered beautiful. But not today.

Sam and Sweets hurried past me as I made my way to the centre of the ruins. Their pale faces easily discernible in the semi-darkness; the body that they bore on the stretcher between them was thankfully covered.

It was later revealed to me that Jones had volunteered for watch duty that night and, unwitnessed, had sat at the centre of the stone disc and slit his own throat. It still makes me shudder to think about it.

The glyphs beneath my feet shone darkly as I crossed to join my crew. The grooves now filled with freshly spilt blood. And there was a lot of it, the whole design now standing out in dark relief. I noticed Nyx's red pupils were flaring brighter than usual at the spectacle.

I later discovered that there was no obvious reason for Jones's unexpected suicide; his psychological evaluation had been sound. One can only presume that the powers that haunted this place penetrated and possessed his mind. I guess we'll never know for sure.

The atmosphere, since the recent blood offering, was seething now, like a living thing. And Jackson had his hat jammed on tight in response.

My team stood in silent expectation as the special ops team checked and double-checked their equipment. I had left behind the headset I had been issued with, as had the others. I just got a very strong feeling that certain equipment was going to malfunction down there, and I could do without the extra distraction. The guns were equipped with torches anyway, so at least I wasn't going to be left in the dark. Well, that's if they functioned!

A deep resonant bass note had also become audible, slowly increasing in volume since we had gathered, filling the air and silencing everyone.

I glanced over at Jackson, his mouth a tight white line, his jaw set. The others were unreadable, as what little light the brightening horizon offered suddenly dimmed and faded.

I located Anastassia amongst the huddled soldiers and gave her a nod, which she acknowledged with a forced smile.

But wait! I did a quick headcount again while I could still make out everyone's silhouette. There was one extra body, standing at the centre of the disc.

Jackson, who had shuffled to my side, leant in close and whispered in my ear. 'Ix.'

I strained my eyes in the gloom, barely able to detect the female figure in our midst. But she must have sensed my scrutiny, because she turned to stare at me just before everything went black.

At the time, I couldn't tell whether the image of her skull was painted or tattooed over her features. Or if it was something more intrinsic to her nature, as it appeared to shift like a holographic image.

You remember those pictures that when you turn them from left to right the image shifts and moves? Well, the effect was very similar to that, or an x-ray.

It was hard to focus, hard to be sure.

Then everything stopped. The sound, any sense of motion, even thought, and then I actually did lose consciousness.

10

I wasn't the only one, although I was still a little embarrassed. I haven't done that since I drank that whole bottle of Mezcal, and consumed the worm — not recommended! I know I mentioned that I was a non-drinker; I am, now at least, but I've certainly partaken in the past.

I noticed a few other bodies clambering to their feet as well as Jackson, who helped me up. He, too, had succumbed; no-one else on our team had.

Before we go further, I should apologise in advance for my flippancy when confronted with certain situations from here on in. The ride on the freight elevator to hell has shaken me up somewhat. Although to compare what just happened to an elevator ride is a little misleading, as I'm sure we never actually moved, not physically anyway, we're just someplace else.

At least we all made it intact, now with one extra addition. Who was quickly surrounded by a number of the spooked soldiers, guns aimed, safety catches off.

Jackson was quick to step in and calm the situation down before it escalated further. 'Stand down, she's with us.'

Ix acknowledged him with a grateful nod, but appeared to be completely unperturbed by the attention. Mind you, with a countenance like hers, it's hardly surprising.

Her dark complexion was augmented by her slightly sunken cheeks, as were her eyes, giving her outward appearance an even more sinister look. And I got a distinct feeling that wasn't her natural look either. She had obviously been under great pressure and stress, the consequences of which taking a visible toll on her physically, and presumably spiritually as well.

Dressed in what I can only describe as native attire, strings of jade beads hung around her neck. Her chocolate brown skin only enhancing that skull facsimile. Which, now that I could see it properly, was more like I could see beneath her skin, like having x-ray vision. I have to admit it was most disconcerting. She'd receive a lot of candy trick or treating at Hallowe'en.

'She's here to guide us to our destination,' Jackson explained. 'I've already briefed you on how crucial she is regarding our mission here.'

The soldiers backed down, mollified, although a little reluctantly, I thought. They were probably just desperate to shoot something. Even "loud-mouth" Tillson was being rather reserved; at least there were some benefits to being in hell.

So here we all were, the eight of us, reunited for the first time in centuries; the feeling I got was inspirative.

And where was here exactly? Well, beyond the disc on which we were all still gathered was what I can only describe as a battlefield, or the aftermath of one at least.

As far as I could see, in every direction was a plain strewn with bodies; the sky — if it was the sky — hung low above us like an infected bruise. And the smell! I muttered a few words to myself in an attempt to magic up a little fresh air, but I reckon there's not much fresh air here to conjure up. So now what I can smell is ripe decay with a hint of eucalyptus. Not a fragrance any manufacturer would be willing to introduce to their plug-in fragrances range.

I think an unspoken message passed between Jackson and Ix as I noticed them acknowledge something with a small nod; and then we were off, into that mire. I noticed Ix was barefoot as well, her lower legs caked in indescribable sludge — gross! I'm glad I wore my big boots now, but that's another pair of footwear ruined!

My team, I'm proud to say, seem little perturbed by our surroundings. The special ops team, on the other hand, were rather pale as they attempted to keep their stomachs from turning inside out.

We formed two lines behind Ix, who seemed oblivious to all the festering bodies underfoot. And it was just that: even the very ground itself appeared to be composed of dead bodies. Centuries of corpses stacked layer upon layer; wherever I put my feet, they either sank into something disgusting or snapped pieces of bone, making me wince. I must admit I envied Sophia's ability to fly right now. The only one of us capable of rising above all this muck.

Nyx had caught up with Ix, but I can't make out whether they're having a conflab or not? Ix is navigating this landscape of the dead with an ease that suggests that she has done this on numerous occasions, inured to the expansive decay over the centuries. Nyx's shadow form is also allowing her certain ease of movement across the uneven ground.

Whereas I'm getting a bit bogged down in this body swamp. Jackson keeps a hold of me, helping when he can, but I reckon the contact is helping him as much as his strong arm is helping me.

I pause for a second to shake a piece of skull off that has lodged onto my boot. 'This place is disgusting.'

'This place,' Mist says reverently, 'was intended as a place of repose for the freshly dead before being guided onwards to Valhalla.'

That's her Nordic version of heaven. In which case, what the…? Did She do this? And for what purpose?

We plod on for a further half-hour? Two? Three? I have no idea. I just blanked out what was under my feet, telling myself it was just mud and sticks and stones. I kindled my power up a little to see if I could detect an end to this place. Apparently not; it is endless. Wow! That's a lot of dead bodies. And if this place is indeed infinite, then where in the hell is Ix taking us?

I'm just about to broach the subject of my rapidly diminishing faith in our guide with Jackson when something clutches at my leg. I almost took off and joined Sophia.

As unexpected as this was, I should have expected it. Noticing now that everyone else was having the same experience. Much of the special ops team roaring and shouting, making the air as fragrant with expletives as it was ripe with the odour of the dead, or undead, as they had all decided to wake up.

Tremendous!

Here we were in the middle of a swamp of dead folks, and all I could think of was: I wish I'd picked a flamethrower.

Shots were fired as skeletal arms grasped and torsos were dragged free of the mire.

'Form a circle, quickly!' Sophia commanded from above, and we complied as fast as those sticky bony fingers and marshy ground would allow.

As soon as we were gathered, I cast a dome around us, Jackson channelling energy to me, strengthening the shield.

Once we were safely interred, or safer, as it still left the matter of the crawling dead within the dome with us. But between the troops, Mist and Kal, they kept them at bay so I could concentrate.

Sophia took up a position directly above us and

drew her sword. I didn't see exactly what happened then; I was too focused on holding the shield. But there was a blaze of fiery light that lasted several seconds completely enveloping us, like a flare exploding. Then, like a light switch being flipped, it was over.

I dropped the shield immediately, keen to escape the confines of our protective shell because, despite everyone's best efforts, it's hard to dispatch the dead, and they were very persistent.

Everyone followed, thankful to feel that charred, lifeless ground beneath their feet. Sophia's divine light had scorched the earth for quite some considerable distance, leaving a small disc of putrescence at the centre where we had huddled together.

You'll notice the severe lack of dialogue here. Well, that's because there wasn't much conversation going on, except for the rather impressive stream of expletives, many of which I'm sure I haven't heard before and would make pretty tedious reading. But in defence of the troops, they were well and truly freaked out. I was a little freaked out myself, but that little victory of ours had certainly bolstered me.

'Here.'

It's Nyx. She and Ix appear to have found something nearby. The going is easier over the charcoaled remains, but I'm wary, and the rest of the plain is still a writhing nightmare.

Nyx calls upon her strength to lift and heave aside

a stone plinth or slab that Ix has led us to.

One of few words is Ix. Then again, she's had nobody for company but the dead for centuries, and so far, they don't seem very talkative or hospitable.

I look to Jackson, in case he's in some kind of psychic communication with her, and he obliges.

'She knows the hidden pathways and secret gates. She has travelled these routes for centuries. It'll be okay.'

He smiles at me and squeezes my hand as Nyx finally heaves the heavy stone slab aside and it hits the ground with a loud thud. Now if that didn't wake everyone here, then they certainly will be now. And they seem to be doubling their efforts to reach us across the tract of blackened ground.

'How the hell did you know that was there?' Tillson demands. He couldn't keep his mouth shut for long.

'You should conserve your breath for when the screaming begins.' Ix finally talks, her voice accented and husky. It would actually be quite attractive under different circumstances.

I don't know whether to shake her hand at the effect her reply has on Tillson or grab her by the shoulders and shake her, demanding what she means by: "when the screaming begins".

Well, he's speechless, and most of the troops have gone a shade somewhere between snow white and that shade of green you find on unripe bananas. Anastassia's sticking close to Mist as we line up to enter the exit that has now been revealed, probably finding a bit of succour being in such proximity to a goddess.

That considered we mixed up our numbers as we leave the fields of the dead and proceed down the staircase of doom. Indiana Jones, where are you now? As the slab has revealed a set of steps that disappear into the darkness below.

This isn't good; if it wasn't for the crawling dead up here, I may have been tempted to stay. But Ix and Nyx are off; they both seem unaffected by it all. You'd think they were just taking a stroll through Central Park.

She still can't work my microwave, though!

The steps soon come to an end and a shuddersome-looking tunnel now stretches out before us. So, guns unholstered, torches on.

I found myself with Jackson, sandwiched between Big K and Chow. First time I've been happy to be near Big K — he almost fills the passage behind me. I'm putting up trip-wires as I go. Magic ones, stretching them between those cold, clammy walls. I don't want the living-dead sneaking up on us. But since we entered this realm, I've got the feeling that they are unable to follow us here. Is that just the rules? Or is there other stuff down here? Worse stuff?

Jackson's taken his hat off, so it's getting serious!

We trudge on in silence for a while until a holler from up ahead echoes within the enclosed space.

'Hey, X, you okay at the rear?'

I think it sounds like Mel; that Scottish twang is unmistakable.

'Yeah, he's cool. X likes it at the rear!' Pampers answers for him from a couple of positions behind me.

'Fuck you, man!'

Ah, a little bit of banter to soothe the nerves. At least morale is picking up again. Still, I don't fancy X's position much.

'Hey, Alice, you couldn't throw up a portal and get us out of here, could you?' Big K asks me.

'Sorry.' I did see if it was possible, but the energy here seems to be suppressing that ability. 'We're stuck here.' It's like pressing the button on a remote control with no batteries in it.

'Shit!'

I have to agree with Big K on that one.

Suddenly, I feel that hair-plucking sensation on my scalp. We're being tracked.

'Something's behind us.' I stop.

'Hey, X! Watch you're six.' Big K delivers the warning.

There's a slight pause. 'Can't see anything. Wait, could be something. I can't make out what it is yet.'

'What's the hold-up back there?' Tillson's dulcet tones join in.

He's upfront, still trying to look as if he's in charge. I almost forgot, just so you know, my gut feeling was right, those fancy headsets — useless. All the internal circuitry was fried, hence all the shouting.

'We got incoming, sir!'

'Who's rear-guard?'

'X, sir, and Sanchez.'

At that moment, I hear X shouting something unintelligible a split second before the rattle of machine-gun fire. Conversation is impossible over the noise. Maddie then pushes her way back down the line towards the rear.

'X? Can you hear me?' Tillson bellows.

He's got a pair of lungs on him. Better yet, why doesn't he get his ass down here instead of relying on one of my crew?

'He's gone! X is gone!'

'What do you mean, gone?'

Not too bright, Tillson! Where do you think he's gone? Just nipped off to buy us all an ice-cream cone?

'I don't know what the hell it was, it just grabbed him and backed off. But I can see it moving, sir. I think it's coming back.'

Another short burst of gunfire.

Sanchez sounds distraught. I hold my breath. Jackson has focused all his attention towards the rear of the line, his brow glistening with beads of perspiration. Then, all of a sudden, it's over. Jackson eases his grip on my hand and the blood flows back.

'It's over,' Maddie calls up ahead.

'Sanchez, you okay?' There's a few seconds' pause — please, not the cook. 'Yes, yes, I'm good.'

But poor old X. We're one down already.

I make a hasty decision and pull Jackson with me to the rear as the line begins to move again. We've not got time to mourn our loss.

The three of us, including Maddie, who remains with us, now form a rear-guard. I'm hanging on to Jackson; it's like together we're stronger, like two cells making a battery.

I get a glimpse of what took X before we continue onwards. It's now the same colour as the stone walls. It fills the tunnel completely.

Have you ever seen footage of those massive boring drills they use to create tunnels through solid rock? Its surface covered with teeth designed for chewing through the stone. Well, if you can imagine that, but more disgusting, with a squid-like beak at the centre and surrounded by tentacles. At least nothing can sneak up on us now. But another thing's for sure, too: there's no going back now either.

The banter doesn't resurface as we march on in silence. And I keep thinking of those movies where the characters return victorious from their quest, perhaps a team member short. And you think that's not very realistic. Well, I'm thinking, are any of us going to make it back victorious? And is that what's important here? As long as we complete our mission, that's what's important. That and I wish I'd brought some chocolate with me and that I'd completed watching that boxset, only two episodes to go! Now I'll never know who the murderer was!

I notice Jackson is concentrating on something before revealing what it is. He's communicating with those at the front of the line.

'Ix has just informed me that each of these stages are trials set up by Her. To test us individually and as a team. Now that She has become aware of our presence, She is constantly reconfiguring the architecture of this place.'

'And to thin our numbers,' Maddie adds grimly.

He nods.

Terrific!

So, essentially, She's just playing with us, and our guide is just as disorientated as the rest of us. I dread to think what it'll be like when She gets serious and stops playing around. Like cats playing with mice, and we both know the consequences of that!

We continue on for several more despondent minutes, before Jackson relays a little positive news.

'There's a chamber up ahead.'

At last. I'm not one who suffers from claustrophobia, but this oppressive tunnel is testing my boundaries. Heights, well, that's different, and clowns. Put me on a clifftop with a clown and I'm done for!

The line picks up speed at the thought of a little

more breathing room and we explode into a massive cathedral-like cave, the domed ceiling arching high overhead.

The interior is adequately lit by balls of light that hover eerily above sconces secured to the walls, and we douse our light sources before regrouping, Ix, at the centre, to await her indispensable guidance. And that's a worrying consideration, because as far as I can make out there's no obvious way out of here. And the tunnel we just entered by? Removed; what a surprise!

Ix studies the interior of the chamber. She appears to be searching for some sort of exit, the skull beneath her Mayan features turning a full three hundred and sixty degrees, as we all study her in turn, waiting for some sort of inspiration.

Even Nyx appears to be stymied for once. I'm getting more than a little apprehensive now as Ix fails to communicate any assurances, and I can sense the troop's nervousness permeating through me as the seconds rack up.

Then the chamber is filled with pandemonium.

11

A sound like thousands of screaming souls in terrible anguish assaults our senses.

I clasp my free hand over one ear, but to no avail; it's as if the noise is inside me. Nobody has escaped its devastating effect, as, one by one, we collapse under the barrage.

I locate Ix and witness a semi-transparent membrane materialise around her. She presses her palms flat against the interior and I read the apology in her eyes just before that cocoon fades away, carrying Ix with it.

The ground's shaking now in conjunction with the reverberation of that choral chaos.

My vision is blurring. All I can feel is Jackson hanging on to me for dear life. Instinctually, I reach out and grab someone's ankle; it's Mist. I'm not letting go — I'm not losing anyone else.

The very chambers of my heart are filled with that infernal noise until it is fit to burst.

Then, as suddenly as it commenced, everything goes quiet. My ears buzz intensely in the silence. Like the aftermath of a really loud rock concert — Rob

Zombie, Detroit, 2006 — now that was loud!

I tentatively open my eyes. Part of me doesn't want to know, but I have to be prepared just in case. At least I'm not alone: Jackson and Mist are with me, and Jackson has Maddie clasped tightly in his other hand.

'You can release my ankle now.'

'Sorry.' I let go of Mist and she rubs her ankle. I *was* squeezing really tight.

We get to our feet and examine our new surroundings. I'd like to say they've improved, but they haven't.

The four of us have been transported to a forest. An ancient, creaky forest. The kind of place that if trolls, orcs, goblins and the gingerbread house the witch from Hansel and Gretel lived in existed, they'd be right at home here.

They don't exist, by the way, in case you wondered. The other things and gingerbread houses; witches do.

There were no signs of life, no bird song or insects calling between themselves. Just the creaking of ancient wood and the dripping of fetid water mixed in with the ringing in my ears. It was creepy.

It took us a few minutes to get re-orientated and bring our weapons to hand, the ringing finally dissipating to a level where we could communicate properly.

And what of the others? I'll fill you in on what became of them later.

It had been our physical contact that had guaranteed we had all been transported together. It was just a theory for now. But one that later proved to be correct.

'Now what?' I was hoping Jackson might be able to dispense some wise words gleaned from Ix before she was spirited away.

'She took her, Ix. I sensed Her fury filling that place before She kidnapped her.'

'So, She was grieved at our ability to navigate Her world and removed our only hope of finding our way through this place.'

Thanks, Mist, I feel much better.

'An egress will be disclosed when we have met Her challenge,' Maddie informs us.

Ix said so much herself. That each new challenge was set to test us.

'She is toying with us. Then meet us head-on, challenge us!' Mist shouts, releasing her frustration.

Not quite sure I want to throw down the gauntlet so soon.

'But Mist is right, which means that She fears us, or why else would She disperse our numbers?' Maddie agrees.

'Then supply me with adversaries and I will dispatch them with pleasure.' Mist raises her voice as she swings her axe. There's no holding her back now. She's separated her from her new buddy.

The axe embeds itself deeply in the trunk of the

nearest tree, the blade cutting deep. She pulls it free and repeats the stroke… and again.

I turn to Maddie, who is standing back with her arms folded, eyebrows raised above her mirrored lenses. Well, we're not going to get very far at this rate.

I wrinkle my nose in disgust: the wound in the tree is leaking something other than sap and smells worse.

'Something's coming,' Jackson whispers.

The three of us turn in the direction he has indicated. Mist is still too focused on lumberjacking to notice.

Jackson pulls on his hat. Must be bad.

'It's like acid in my brain,' he explains.

I sympathise. I've had a few mornings like that, usually as a result of cocktail consummation the night before.

The ground quakes beneath our feet and even Mist stops to face the as-yet-unseen threat. Then the sodden ground heaves and splits open ahead of us and a multitude of writhing, thrashing tentacles burst forth and dance with a sickening frenzy.

I don't think bullets are going to help much here, so I holster my guns.

Note to self: next time (hope there isn't a next time) choose the flamethrower.

Instead, between myself and Jackson we attempt to constrain the thrashing, while Mist leaps into action again.

We all see what she's planning and we all step aside as she makes short work of the softwood. And watch with a certain amount of satisfaction as it crashes down right on target, crushing the unsightly thrashing. A few stick out and twitch like proverbial spiders' legs, before lying still.

Just as I'm about to congratulate Mist on her felling skills, Jackson spoils the moment.

'It's not over.'

Of course it isn't! What was I thinking?

Things then start falling from the canopy. They look a bit like hands, but with tiny snapping jaws at the end of each finger — a lovely touch — and they appear to have too many fingers than is normally allowed. And suddenly the forest is filled with them.

Oh well, here goes!

I grab a gun and empty a full clip without hitting one. I snap in another clip like I was taught, and empty it without striking a bullseye again. Sorry, no cuddly toy this time.

I holster my gun and instead stomp a branch off the tree Mist felled; it gives with a little magical push. I was always quite good at baseball, and I commence to bat, sending several spinning into nearby trees with a satisfying splat. The odd one grabs hold of my bat with biting fingers, but I soon batter it to a pulp on a tree trunk.

Jackson, his hat's off, go Jackson! He's using

telekinesis; he's pretty good at it as well, to send these horror hands flying into the trees and the far distance.

Soon we fall into a rhythm, him pitching and me batting. I'm almost beginning to enjoy this.

Mist never seems to miss her mark and the bisected remains of hands lie littered around her. Maddie's pile of stone hands is equally impressive. Her skills are modifying because these things definitely don't have any eyes. Unless she's just unlocking her full powers, that have previously lain dormant?

Jackson's getting into the swing of it now, pitching for all three of us. This is getting too easy.

Hang on, I shouldn't have nurtured that thought. What was the name of that Ray Bradbury novel? *Something Wicked This Way Comes* — that was it. Well, here it comes!

The hands dwindle in number and finally disappear as trees shudder and crack as something pushes its way through the forest towards us.

I notice the stench first. Why does the underworld have to smell so bad? Like stagnant water and sewage. Which could be seen as a positive, as the creature can't be: it's invisible.

Pieces of detritus cling to its form as it lumbers onward, and I can't give you a fitting description except that it's big, if the indentations it leaves in the sodden ground are anything to go by. The round, elephant-like prints quickly fill with murky water. And judging by their number, it has several feet.

Before any of the rest of us can fully react, Mist launches her axe and it spins through the air with phenomenal force to embed itself solidly in an area that could be the creature's head. There's a moment's pregnant silence as the creature decides what to do, before finally committing itself to dying, and it keels over with a crash that matches that of the earlier felled tree, forcing a miasma of putrescent water into the air. A shower of broken branches and diseased-looking leaves flutter down in its wake.

Mist strides over, clambering over the felled beast to retrieve her axe, only to plunge it in, again and again, just to be sure.

The number of times I've watched a movie where someone dispatches the bad guy, or so they think, and you just know that they're going to make a comeback. What's the tag-line to that zombie film? Ah, yes: "double-tap". Or in Mist's case, numerous taps. I'm glad it's invisible now so I can't see the carnage as she re-joins us.

'What was it?' I ask, my curiosity getting the better of me. Mist might have a better idea after getting up close and personal with it, especially with the settling mist of water coating it.

'Ugly.'

Fair enough. I've had a few dates over the years which invisibility on their part would have been a distinct bonus.

'And our way out is revealed,' Jackson announces, smiling a genuine smile again.

It's nice to see: he's got a nice smile and I can't help but smile in return.

He points over my shoulder and I realise I'm just smiling at him before turning around, a little embarrassed, to see what he's pointing at.

A door, just standing there in the forest. Solid wood with a brass knob.

'Shall we?' Maddie is first to make a move and lead us to salvation, or onto the next horror show.

Now, I've got an image in my head of some screaming demon filling the doorway on the other side, all teeth and insatiable appetite. Or a Jehovah's Witness on a crusade to personally lead me to salvation.

I'm not opening it.

It's Mist that turns the handle and opens it wide, while I point my gun at whatever's on the other side.

12

A change of perspective, I think. As I survived the revelation of that door and as I wasn't present to dispense a first-hand account of the plight of the others, I later plied them with questions, extracting what details I could so I could compile their experiences and relate them to yourself.

Next are Kal and Anastassia. I did remember to ask, and it was physical touch that determined who was translocated with whom, as Kal did indeed scoop up Anastassia when we were assaulted.

Now picture the scene:

A Roman amphitheatre which is littered with corpses, old and new. The expectant crowd made up of the dead; no surprises there! But for dead people, they were very noisy and enthusiastic, apparently.

Around the circumference of the arena were six apertures through which something monstrous came careening towards them moments after they had appeared.

I asked for details. I know, I'm a glutton for punishment.

Anastassia compared one to a rhinoceros, but with

its skin flayed and too many legs; something leech-like that kept folding in on itself to reveal endless razor teeth; what appeared to be a mass of fused people, which could propel itself in any direction at speed with its numerous arms and legs; and what she could only describe as someone's attempt at constructing a robot with human bones, scraps of festering flesh still attached.

She threw her arms up in the air after that and muttered something in Russian and walked off. I didn't pursue the matter further.

I think we got lucky with the biting hands, but despite the odds, you can guess the result. This was bread and butter to Kal. And this wasn't Anastassia's first rodeo either, although she did use up all her ammunition on the ball of fused people and the leech-thing. After that, she kept close to Kal; it was up to her to defend them both now.

The fifty-calibre despatched the peeled rhino and the bone robot, having to resort to her swordwomanship (don't know if that's actually a word? But it should be!) to chop the remaining things into inactivity as the gun whirred on empty. The last construct taking several decapitations to still it.

How many heads did that thing have?

They then made their escape via one of the apertures the creatures had entered the arena through and turned up...

Well, we'll get there soon enough.

The special ops team were largely transported together, as they were tightly grouped when we were struck in that chamber. And I'm sad to report that they didn't fare so well. Only Sanchez and Big K made it out alive. Someone who can make a curry that good deserves a second chance.

So, no more are Pampers, Chow and Thumper. I should mention at this point I had earlier assumed that Thumper was so-called because he thumped people. Apparently not. When he was a child, he had a pet rabbit called Thumper, after the one in *Bambi*. I could never have called that; it was Mel that told me later.

Anyway, they turned up in the middle of a blizzard and, despite their best attempts, got separated. Then the creatures appeared.

'They were like yeti had got it on with a polar bear.'

Nice image, Big K. It was him who filled me in on the details while we were still in the underworld. I was trying to get him to focus and calm down. I don't think him reliving these moments helped.

'They just appeared out of all that snow, like ghosts. One of them punched clean through Pampers. I could actually see right through him! Shit, man, I ain't ever seen anything like that before. And I've seen some shit. We just panicked, scattered. What the fuck else could we do? Bullets were useless. It was Pampers who had the thrower, and he was toast.'

These are quotes, by the way, so excuse the florid language. And we had a flamethrower? And he never used it? Maybe if one of my crew had been transported with them, we could have rescued more? Who knows? Back to Big K's transcript.

'We just kept moving, me and Sanchez. I could hear something behind us. Chow had somehow found us. But Thumper — you should have heard the screams.' He took a moment here to take a drink as I did my best to console him, but he was shaken up pretty bad. It would've taken a lifetime of therapy to just get him through the worst of it. And this guy could've given a grizzly a run for its money. Not that bears are renowned for their financial insolvency.

'We ran into this wall, solid ice, but you could see through it kinda, like glass. Sanchez is yelling that there's movement out there; we were trapped. Chow starts pounding at that wall with her launcher.'

And we had a grenade launcher? Although, to be fair, I don't think there was ever much of an opportunity to use it previously with any real effectiveness.

'She's pounding this wall and there's ice spraying everywhere, and then we were through. The hole was still blocked; a chunk of ice had fallen down, so I take a run and put my shoulder to it. The piece just breaks off and I go through with the momentum. Sanchez is right at my ass and I drag her through. Then it's Chow.' He pauses for a sip of water. 'I grab her with both hands, but then one of those things grabs her from behind and starts dragging her back. I'm pulling real hard, but she starts screaming and I can feel her tearing apart. I can actually feel it!' He holds his hands up in front of his face in disbelief.

I halt proceedings there; he's been through enough, there's no need to extract more details. Chow didn't make it, but without her, Sanchez and Big K wouldn't have made it either.

Now onto Nyx, Tillson and Mel.

I initially approached Mel regarding their experience as Tillson wasn't there to ask. Sorry, kind of gave away the ending there, but all I got was:

'I dinae ken, it was too fuckin' dark.'

So I asked Nyx; her ability to see in the dark was a distinct boon then and is what probably saved Mel in the end.

They materialised on a narrow path clinging to the side of a mountain. Unscalable height above, yawning precipice below. The three of them had to shuffle along until they reached a bridge.

When I say shuffle, two of them did; for Nyx, it was more of a casual saunter. And I say bridge: she described it as one of those you see on documentaries about indigenous people in South America or Asia, spanning ravines using the most basic of materials. Those rickety constructions that you say to yourself — no way! I would, anyway; as I've said, I'm not a fan of heights.

Nyx was perfectly aware this was a trap, but they had little option than to continue onwards, the whole journey in complete darkness: not even the torches could cut a swathe through that pitch. So, not much fun for Tillson and Mel.

With Nyx guiding them, though, they crossed successfully and found themselves at the entrance to a mountain pass, cliffs on either side. This is where the ambush occurred.

Nyx's description of their attackers is vague due to the intense light that radiated from their eyes. Although Nyx doesn't mind daylight, it does her no physical harm (direct contact with divine light, on the other hand, is another matter. It was my shield earlier that protected her from Sophia's blast that devastated the dead), but she does function better at night. And the suddenly focused beams after the all-consuming darkness did disorientate her. All she recalled was tall, wraith-like figures that formed from the shadows in the rock, their eyes blazing suns, their fingers needle-like talons.

I thought perhaps Mel might be able to add a detail or two with the addition of light at this stage, but what he said was:

'Like fuckin' headlights, man, full-beam, ye ken?'

I'm not sure that I did.

Nyx is quick and strong, and despite the blinding lights she managed to avoid those talons, telling me that they snapped very easily, like twigs. A twig to her would be a branch to you and me.

Whilst she was snapping, Mel managed to shoot one down, the light from the muzzle flashes guiding his aim and avoiding Nyx.

Tillson wasn't so lucky and took one of those clusters of talons right in the chest. Nyx verified his passing once the attack was repelled.

The exit turned out to be hidden in a crevice in the rock face that opened up and led them to safety. After Big K's emotional report, Nyx's emotionless matter-of-fact disclosure left me a little dumbfounded. Nothing seems to faze that woman at all.

Sophia was the only one out of all of us who was relocated alone. Probably because she had taken to the wing and no-one could grab hold of her.

Her venue was a void. Just grey nothing. She just had to hold her position and wait.

As she said, there was no sense of up or down, left or right. She felt completely disorientated. It was then, when she was feeling most vulnerable, that the attack came, from every conceivable direction.

'Scraps of life, abattoir detritus, infused with sentience not fit for human eyes.'

She's very intelligent, Sophia, and can be quite eloquent in her choice of words sometimes.

'Their numbers innumerable. I was overwhelmed.'

It sounded just offal. I'm sorry, I couldn't resist!

Anyway, perseverance, and the administration of divine light and sword skills with finesse — I couldn't imagine her dispensing sword skills in any other way — eventually saw her through. But judging by the streaks of unsightly muck that daubed her skin and clung to her hair, it must have been quite an assault.

I gave her a big hug on being reunited with her, despite the gunk. She had quelled the attack single-handed and I could see beneath that somewhat aloof veneer that she draped herself in, that the ordeal had deeply affected her. To be isolated from her friends and have to stand alone, I don't think I could have handled that.

She was so intent on repelling the hordes that she had little recollection of how exactly she had arrived here; but reunited we were, what was left of us anyway, and that was the main thing.

And where exactly was here?

13

Despite the length of time we each individually spent separated from each other, we all arrived synchronously. In a room, just an ordinary room, without any idea about how we had arrived. It was like coming out of a drug fugue. I mean, I remember Mist opening that door — what I just can't recall is walking through the doorway, and we're all the same.

We took a hiatus before continuing, the direction we were to take quite obvious as the room, square with bare walls and floorboards — and a rather nauseating water feature fabricated into one of the walls; but it wasn't water and I'm quite sure cherubs aren't meant to be doing that! — only possessed one door and we're in no rush to open it. We were secure in here for now. One way in, one way out. We even had light, that light shade, though; a paper lantern which was distasteful enough, but it was what was staining it that concerned me. But, all in all, quite comfortable considering what we had just survived.

Besides, Big K was in no fit state to continue at this point. Sanchez and Mel were holding up, but were grateful for the respite. I took this opportunity to get Big

K's take on his recent experience, of which I've just related. Sanchez was happy to let him unburden himself while she chewed listlessly on a protein bar. Mel and Jackson also indulged, but I was too stressed to eat. The others, well, as I said before, I think it's more a novelty thing for them; they can, but they don't have to. I can't be one hundred percent as I've never actually asked, it just never occurs to me. Because if I put food out, they eat (especially my pancakes and maple syrup); doesn't mean they need it.

Just listen to myself, I'm rambling now; it's that door looming before me. I get a distinct feeling that we'll finally confront Her once we cross the threshold. I'm nervous; not like a job interview or first date nervous, but I'm stepping into the ring with the entire wrestling elite kind of nervous.

But consummate professionals that we are, we rallied onward. From Nyx the personification of serenity, to the opposite end of the scale, Big K, who was so tense I think if I'd tapped him with a hammer he would have shattered, cartoon style.

I'd also like to take advantage of this lull in proceedings to explain my misgivings at this point. I think it's safe to include Jackson in this rhetoric as well.

Despite my long history, much of which has been dispersed now by the passage of time. Gleaning knowledge and remembering, building a foundation for future lives. Practising and enhancing my abilities to better protect myself and prepare for the liberation of my team. Jackson as well has been similarly burdened.

My magical skills involving sorcery, manipulation, obfuscation, and more recently portal casting, although very proficient, still leave me feeling woefully unqualified for this kind of assignment. But to be fair on myself, would anyone feel sanguine enough in a situation such as this?

And in particular, in this current existence, I have endeavoured to attempt to savour the lighter things in life and not dwell on the past. Hence, my often-flippant attitude and outwardly callow persona. I can assure you that is not, in fact, the case; I've just come to embrace that aspect of myself and nourish it; it's what has essentially kept me centred and sane (relatively speaking!) over the many, many decades I've been slowly piecing myself back together. And unlike the others, the immortals amongst us, which is a bit of a misnomer as they, too, can die under certain conditions. Myself and Jackson most assuredly can, and I for one don't want to have to start from scratch again, so to speak; my soul is just too weary for such a daunting assignment.

Essentially, what I have strived to achieve during this lifetime is live what society would deem a "normal life". Well, there you have it. And to sum it all up: I'm bricking it!

And I've just noticed that Kal's sporting a minor

injury; that's also made me a little anxious as well. One of her upper arms has been slashed, a dribble of purple blood now streaking her bicep. Which reinforces my previous statement about immortals not being immortal! But she is unfazed. A "flesh wound"? She shrugs it off and prepares to continue onwards.

We do weapons checks; well, not much for me to check: two pistols, one empty — check.

What was empty is discarded or reloaded, and Sanchez hands one of her pistols to Anastassia. Oh yes, I did ask Sanchez while we were preparing for the onset — Big K was in no frame of mind for further questioning — why Pampers hadn't torched those abominable polar things? She said he tried, but the flammable liquid had frozen. It would appear that She had considered this and perhaps that was why She had conjured a polar environment to thwart that attack. Which means that Her machinations and therefore Herself were indeed vulnerable.

So, except for a few sidearms, four assault rifles, ammunition, and, of course, Kal's grenade necklace — that was something, at least — we were almost reduced to blades and prayer. But pray to whom? The goddess? Which one? The ones that mattered were with me. And She was completely off her trolley.

Considering what armaments we had gathered, in any other situation — yay! — here, not so much.

'Are we ready to continue?' Nyx asks, overseeing

proceedings.

'No,' comes Big K's predictable reply.

Everybody ignores him and gathers themselves behind Nyx as she prepares to open the door. Big K reluctantly joins us; I think he's more terrified of being left alone than accompanying us through there.

She gradually pulls open the door to reveal a dystopian nightmare.

14

Big K freaked out immediately and was summarily silenced with a resounding slap from Sanchez.

'Get it together, big man; we can do this, okay? Remember Afghanistan?' She held out her fist, waiting for the customary fist-bump, which he rather reluctantly obliged her with. His sweating bald head was now painted with a rather impressive handprint. 'You okay? You got this?'

'Yeah, yeah, I got this, Sanchez.'

He was like a little boy being scolded.

Good for you, Sanchez. Although, to be honest, I didn't rate his chance of survival too highly.

The rest of us were as ready as could be expected. Jackson looked particularly concerned, and I correctly guessed what was troubling him.

'Ix?'

'Yeah, I'm worried about her.'

'We'll find her. I've broken out goddesses before, remember.' I try to kindle a little confidence in him. But I don't know how successful I've been, and I was more than a little concerned about her well-being myself.

Once we had crossed the threshold into this fresh

hell, a glance over my shoulder confirmed what I'd already been expecting. The doorway and the room we'd just left were both gone. No going back now; tremendous, the story of my life.

Now, how to describe this place?

A city, a bit like the one in *Blade Runner*, but worse in every respect. *Silent Hill* — have you seen that? When the town transforms and goes all to hell when that siren wails. I'd say that's a pretty apt description. Curse my penchant for horror movies; now I'm imagining all kinds of slithering, crawling nasty stuff lurking in the shadows.

Big K looks as if I were to whisper boo to him, he'd drop from a coronary. Anastassia and Sanchez are being professional, but you can see how tense they are. Mel's on point with Maddie and Nyx; he's doing all right, as are the rest of my crew.

Our target is a tower that soars above the pollution and decay, which appears to lie central amidst all the muck and filth. There are heaps of garbage lying in piles and strewn across the pathways that criss-cross this city. Some I recognise as biological remains; human or animal, it's hard to be sure, but I don't linger to find out what exactly. And hairless rat-looking creatures scurry about feeding, their features a little too human for my liking.

Actually, to call this edifice a tower is probably a bit misleading. It's more like a raised platform. The top completely flat, with something floating above it. It's hard to make out any specific details at this distance. But I just know it's Her. I can feel it, the power emanating from that place. And that's where Nyx is leading us, so I guess it's just a case of reaching our destination in one piece.

With three upfront, I'm grouped with Kal, Mist and Sophia, who has taken to gliding just above the ground (I wouldn't walk through that filth either if I didn't have to). Anastassia, Big K and Sanchez are sandwiched in the middle.

I can feel Her scrutiny. She's very aware of our presence, been expecting us probably since we first travelled to this cursed place. Or at least since Ix guided us past the fields of the dead. Toying with us, although I suspect She was eager to dispense with the special ops; that was probably an added addition She hadn't accounted for.

I'm leaving my usual trip-wires in our wake. The invisible spider silk charms cling to the crumbling walls and wave languidly in the fetid air. At least their application means I can relax, a tiny bit at least. But then there are still the possibilities of unexpected assaults from the front, left and right. Oh, and from above and below, of course.

This is giving me a headache.

'You picking anything up?' I ask Jackson. Anything to break this unbearable silence.

'I'm getting readings in every direction, like something prodding at my brain, looking for a way in.'

He's struggling to keep Her out and the hat's been jammed back on his head. I take his hand and squeeze, which seems to help both of us, so I hang on. It's a nice feeling, comforting.

I see Mel's fist punching the air up ahead, military-speak for "halt". Everybody complies. What's going on? No-one's speaking.

I notice Jackson stare up ahead with an intensity that says he can see or at least feel a presence. I catch a ride, psychically, and I sense it, too. It's big.

We pull ourselves into a tighter formation, but still allow each other enough room to manoeuvre as we prepare to defend ourselves.

I can see it now with my own eyes. But it's hard to make out too much detail, it numerous legs seem to encompass much of its body. Tapping across the ground and walls as it closes in fast. It's the colour of infection.

Maybe I should have brought a tube of antiseptic cream and squirted that at it? Would've taken one hell of a tube, though!

I cast a couple of hastily conjured psychic nets over the entrances to the two alleyways that bisect the street immediately to our rear. Contact with Jackson makes this easy and the magic is potent. I don't want anything sneaking up on us unannounced.

It's close enough now for Maddie's stone stare to

be having some effect, the petrified legs breaking and shattering under the weight of the creature. Just like my developing skills, she's getting good. But it continues to propel itself forward undaunted by its losses, sprouting new legs to replace the ones that have snapped off.

Its legs are splitting open now as it nears, and there are lines and lines of teeth in there. And it's got a lot of legs!

That's when the rattle of machine gun fire fills the air, but that seems to be having little effect.

Jackson and I combine forces and attempt to push it back. We slow it down, but it continues to advance as if pushing through treacle.

Sophia lifts off and, directing energy with her sword, slices through those limbs like butter, bringing it crashing to the ground. But it can sprout them as fast as she's severing them.

Light-bulb moment! I've got an idea. I don't like it one bit, but what other options do we have? Jackson picks it up and gives me a stare as if I'd suggested we go skydiving, but instead of packing a parachute, why don't we pack a picnic instead?

I catch Kal's eye; she's preparing to enter the affray with Mist. 'Your necklace?' I ask.

She removes it and hands it over. I haven't tried to cast a portal since we first arrived, but we'll only be hopping a short distance, and with Jackson plugged in I'm sure I can do this. But that will mean he's coming with me; I'll need the continued energy boost to get back.

I grab him in a bear hug, clutching the string of incendiary grenades in one hand. He grabs tightly onto me and hooks a finger through one of the grenade's pins. It's going to be dark in there.

Note to self: try this hugging again, but without the imminent threat of death by monster looming over us.

I close my eyes and concentrate hard; without my shield and Jackson's telekinetic push, that creature is almost on us. I'll have to make this quick.

The intention is well defined in my mind, and we arrive at our destination and return in mere seconds, covered in the worst, foulest crud you could possibly imagine. No, in fact, you couldn't, be thankful. I threw up. I think Jackson might've fought nausea successfully, but after witnessing my efforts, decided to join in.

I carried us both straight to the heart of that thing, if indeed it had a heart as we would know it. Its central core, whatever was keeping this thing alive. As soon as we appeared, Jackson pulled the pin. I felt the movement at my back, then I got us the hell out of there.

We both missed the explosion as we were bent double, but the muffled explosions, the rending of tearing flesh and the rain of stinking matter were hard to ignore. Thank the goddess my stomach was already empty. Which goddess? I don't know any more. It's just become a force of habit.

It had been a complete success, and now everybody was speckled with monster guts. Don't say I'm not generous. Except for Sophia, who incinerated it before it landed on her, and Nyx, who just shifted into shadow form and back. She's teaching me that when we get back. She looks as fresh now as she did when we left Canada.

'Fucking sweet!'

Ah, Big K, a man who knows just what the occasion calls for. First time I've seen him smile in a while, though.

'I'd hug you,' Mist offers, 'but you're disgusting.'

I look myself over, and yes, Mist has some pieces of stuff on her clothes and in her hair, but she has nothing on me if Jackson's appearance is anything to compare myself by, and I attempt to remove the worst of it before we continue.

My hair! That is going to take so much shampoo and conditioner to put right.

But I've suddenly got more worrying matters on my mind (and let me tell you, the condition of my hair at the moment is very concerning) as that plucking sensation across my scalp refocuses my attention.

Kal! It's only Kal; she's cautiously examining one of the alleyways.

'This one's clear; we can take the next right, and get back on track.'

The substantial bulk of that beast adequately fills the street ahead, and there's no way I'm climbing over it. So, we follow her lead, the order of the team reversing, with Maddie, Nyx and Mel bringing up the rear now.

'Hey, that was really bad-ass.'

'Thanks, Sanchez. So was your curry, by the way.' What the hell am I saying? How can I possibly think of curry right now? Thank the goddess my stomach is cleaned out.

'It's the cinnamon,' she reveals.

'Really? I could never have guessed that.'

'It makes all the difference. It was my grandmother's recipe.'

'Where you from originally?' The accent's familiar, but even combined with her olive complexion I still can't add the two up.

'Colombia. But me and my big brother got out of there with my grandparents when we were little. Ended up in São Paulo, a right shit-hole. I hated it, really missed home. But with drug cartels running wild, it just became too dangerous.' She shrugs.

I don't ask her about her parents. I can guess. 'Where's your brother now?'

'A criminal defence lawyer in DC. Doesn't figure, right?' She smiles, abashed. 'And here's me shooting at monsters in hell!'

I don't know what to say to that and the

conversation dies there, just as Kal brings us to a halt at the next junction.

On the right, the way we need to go if we intend on heading in the direction of the tower, is blocked. The whole street appears to be a breeding ground for some sort of fungoid-looking thing. It thickly carpets the ground and walls, almost filling the street. Its phosphorescent, decidedly noxious appearance means we're definitely not going that way.

Kal approaches the glowing mass and tentatively prods the nearest growth with the tip of one sword. The pod instantly splits open and disgorges a human head, supported by a thin wavering neck. After pinpointing our position, the jaws then split wide — I mean almost in two, like the lid of a box — and hisses through broken decaying teeth.

'I ain't going down there!' Big K states, rather inconsequentially, because there's no way I'm going down there either.

Mel agrees in his inimitable style. 'Ya didnae think any of us thought any different, did ya? Ya big muppet.'

The head fungus sways eerily and its eyes slither out on thin stalks to the sound of other pods splitting open.

I'm thinking of that flamethrower again! Or even a Zippo and a gallon of fuel.

Sophia unfurls her light wings and heads vertically up. I can feel the downdraft from where I'm standing, warm and comforting, aiding my hair to slowly congeal and solidify.

We regather a little distance from the staring heads; they were really beginning to freak me out. She was probably watching us through those eyes.

Sophia's sortie reveals to us more of the same head fungi. We're being conducted along a specific route, which will take us through a particularly rundown-looking building. I'm not particularly enthused about this option — there are too many opportunities for Her to ambush us with Her loathsome conceptions in there.

'We have little option,' Nyx states, after Sophia's impartation. 'We are bound to play by Her rules. For now, at least.'

So, its weapons at the ready, torches on, it's murky in there. Sophia elegantly refolds her wings and bolsters her aura, providing some very welcome comforting light. She doesn't have to accompany us; she could simply employ her aeronautical skills and meet us on the other side. But we're a team, and she wouldn't forsake us now. But still, I appreciate her comforting presence. Leading us on, glowing sword held aloft, like an angelic Joan of Arc.

I should point out that despite Nyx's aversion to concentrated divine light, i.e., the cocoon in which He had her entombed within or the focused beam Sophia can deploy with her sword, Sophia's Seraph aura doesn't harm her in any way. But needless to say,

Sophia is very aware of the situation and she does employ great vigilance when wielding her weapon. So now that's clarified, we keep close-knit as we try to remain within that penumbra of heavenly light; except for Nyx, who melts into the shadows seamlessly, dissolving. She periodically returns, refashioning herself, her face looming out of the darkness, to inform Sophia of which route to lead us on.

It's a good strategy, but Big K's sudden expletives at Nyx's unexpected reappearances are becoming tiresome and putting me on edge. Until Sanchez thumped him into silence.

So, between Sophia's guiding light and Nyx's ataraxy within the darkness…

Ataraxy — the new word for the day. Sorry, I've neglected this a bit; other things on my mind! Meaning a state of serene calmness, self-assuredness. That's Nyx to a tee when she's in her element. Anyway, back to it.

— we were soon confronted with a stairwell that climbed up into the shadows. Nyx conveyed that on the nineteenth floor — and I'd been expecting the thirteenth! — an enclosed walkway would then allow us to cross over to the adjacent building.

I shall dispense with any lavish details regarding the interior of the building, as if you've seen any horror film set in an abandoned hospital or mental institution, then you get the general idea. It was all flickering lights, shifting shadows and chilling wailing. And, of course, there's the addition of piles of feet, just feet, of all sizes and colours and in varying degrees of putrefaction — and they smell awful! Although, bizarrely, we just passed a poster plastered to the wall advertising Justin Bieber's latest tour.

I wonder if he's down here as well?

There appears to be some sort of leakage on one of the floors above, as a constant trickle of ghastly looking fluid dribbles over the steps as we ascend. I say dribbles, as it has the same consistency as saliva. At least it's not blood or something worse; either way, I'm burning these boots when I get home.

Home! How far away that seems now. In fact, everything I'm wearing is going the same way, and I'll even buy Jackson a new hat.

As we approach the nineteenth floor, I can make out a decidedly unsettling slopping sound. What now? And Nyx congeals out of the darkness, her golden irises ablaze in the gloom to inform us of what to expect.

'What's the news, Nyx?' I've got to ask.

Her look conveys everything I need to know and we ready ourselves for what lies through those double-doors.

'The passage between this building and the adjacent one lies approximately two hundred fotmal on our left, once we enter the corridor beyond these doors.'

That didn't help — fotmal? — turns out it is equivalent to about one foot. Nyx never grasped decimalisation or other modern systems of measurement. But I was more concerned about what she disclosed next.

'Once we cut our way through the half-humans.'

'Half-humans! What the…?'

My sentiments exactly, Big K.

She doesn't elaborate.

'Anything we should be particularly concerned about?' Maddie asks her.

Particularly concerned about! Yeah, like everything! But you've got to admire their insouciance.

'You okay?' I check in on Anastassia as she double-checks the pistol Sanchez donated before we enter the corridor. She's been very quiet.

'No.'

I can't argue with that.

'I can't stop shaking,' she confesses.

And I notice it's only her prosthetic that's keeping her gun steady in her grip.

'Getting low on ammo as well. Asides what's in here' — she taps the gun — 'Sanchez gave me a spare clip; then I'll have to rely on this.' She indicates the large blade she has sheathed and strapped to one thigh. 'But I hadn't planned on getting close enough to actually use it.' She smiles humourlessly. 'How about you?'

'I really need a shower.'

'You do stink,' she agrees.

We both refrain from laughing out loud as the situation calls for a more restrained approach, as Nyx shoulders open the door and Sophia glides onward, lighting our way.

'Keep it tight and keep it moving,' Sanchez orders.

Although I think that's more for Big K's benefit than anyone else.

Nyx, Kal, Maddie and Mist enter next, the rest of us close behind.

'Only single shots,' Anastassia reminds those with weapons at the ready. 'We need to conserve ammunition.'

The red laser targeting dots dance across the interior as Sophia blazes her way through the chaos we're suddenly confronted with. Even Big K pulls it together, picking off targets with precision, as we hurry towards our destination.

The corridor is thick with crawling torsos, as they scramble to intercept us. They cling to the walls and hang from the ceiling in their determination to prevent us from proceeding.

Jackson and I combine our talents and push back against them with an invisible wall, creating a corridor within the corridor of bodies.

Kal drops back as a pair of doors are ripped from their hinges further down the corridor behind us, spilling more of these atrocities into the mêlée. Her wind-milling arms and spinning blades reduce them to quivering lumps of flesh.

I spot several cylinders standing beside what appears to be a hospital trolley, and drag Jackson with me to check the contents. Jackson grabs a half-full one when he recognises the symbol for flammable gas printed on the side.

We're approaching our exit now, but the number of torsos is overwhelming. Jackson passes on an image of what we have in mind.

Big K takes the cylinder and launches it deep into the throng of bodies behind us and it disappears from view as the torsos tumble forward like a wave.

We form a compact unit as I shield us from the explosion. It takes a few random shots before someone targets the cylinder in that writhing maelstrom.

The explosion lights up the corridor behind us, throwing body parts in every direction. The shield protects us and bits impact the surface and slide greasily to the floor.

Sophia emits an intense burst of divine light ahead of us, parting the way long enough for us to navigate the rest of the bodies while they are still disorganised after the double blast.

'I'm out,' Anastassia informs us, and Mist keeps close to her, keeping her assailants at bay with great sweeps of her axe.

Maddie is doing her best, but the sheer volume of numbers is getting too much. Nyx is tearing them apart with her bare hands, phasing quickly in and out of her shadow form to move quickly between her intended victims.

Mel manages to reposition himself and throws Anastassia a spare clip. 'Last one.'

'Cheers.' She snaps it in thankfully and resumes her attack, aiding Mist.

Kal takes the lead, chopping like the demon slayer she is, her blue skin daubed with thick, dark blood. None of us is in a much better condition physically; splatters of blood and goddess knows what adorns us all as we finally get to those double-doors, Kal taking out the last of our adversaries. I don't know how she can co-ordinate all those arms and weapons, as she alternates between swords for best effect.

A few more stabs and slashes remove the pustulating horror that crouches directly in front of our exit. This thing would even send H.P. Lovecraft rushing to the toilet to empty his bowels.

And then we're through.

Jackson and I slam those doors closed and exert our will to bar them, while the others face what lies on the other side.

Which is… nothing.

The connective bridge is completely deserted. Even the insistent noise of slithering half-bodies has been silenced. It's eerie.

The team gather at the centre of the crossing and

prepare, as Jackson and I relinquish our hold and hurry to join them.

Nothing happens.

All is silent, the doors remain closed. We wait with bated breath, Anastassia brandishing her blade at my side, her empty weapon discarded. That is one big blade; Mist would like that.

'It is done,' Nyx announces, and as one we relax, a little. 'She can only exact so much of Her will into each segment of this place. She is dispersing Her powers too frivolously with these mindless games.'

Nyx seems to be very well informed about the subject. And now I'm beginning to harbour the possibility that Nyx knows her of old.

She looks me straight in the eye with those golden orbs and gives me an almost imperceptible nod. Looks like I hit the nail on the head with that little inference.

'We should continue before She has the opportunity to marshal Her hordes once more and regain Her stamina. If we exert enough pressure, She will continue to weaken.'

'Well, what are we waiting for?' Big K's surprising enthusiasm in response to Nyx's pep talk rallies us all into action.

A poster on the wall catches my eye just before we exit the bridge and enter the next building. It's Justin Bieber again! But this time someone's scratched out his eyes and drawn on pointy teeth. It's an improvement.

15

We find ourselves, unsurprisingly, confronted with another stairwell. And we descend with all due haste after Nyx's informed spiel.

Typically, Big K leads the charge; or, as it's probably playing out in his mind, the retreat.

We reach ground level without further obstacles and we tumble through the doors into a long corridor lined with closed doors. At the far end, slumped against the wall, is a solitary figure. I get the impression that whatever it is, it's snoozing, awaiting our arrival, and consequently, we traverse the corridor cautiously.

As we approach, I can see the wall against which it is propped is flanked by two revolving doors — the exit. But first, we have to brave this final challenge. She's not allowing us to escape that easily.

I can clearly make out now that the recumbent figure is an obese clown.

Now cover your ears, or cover your eyes, and pardon my French, but...

I hate fucking clowns!

Sorry, but certain situations call for language befitting of the moment. And this clown isn't the kind that you would hire for your five-year-old's birthday bash, as he twitches into life with a sinister animation that makes my skin creep.

He reveals he's bigger than Big K as he clambers to his big clown feet, his painted features drooping on his sloughing skin, his bright red nose a pustule of blood fit to burst.

Big K empties the last of his clip into its chest as the clown grins with broken teeth and launches himself off the wall with a speed that catches us all unprepared. And we dive through the nearest adjacent doors, splitting the team up.

I'm with Jackson — I haven't let go of him since that corridor of torsos — and Anastassia. The room resembles that of an office, with desk, swivel chair, filing cabinet and some rather unusual and nauseating items nailed to the wall in place of pictures. It looks like Damien Hirst won the contract to supply this company with their office artwork.

Jackson drags me over to the floor-to-ceiling window and places his free palm flat against the glass, which is already smeared with bloody handprints. He focuses his psychic ability, and the pane almost immediately starts to vibrate.

The clown has decided to target us first. Why couldn't he chase Big K? He's the one that shot him! And on discovering his bulk is preventing him from fitting through the doorway, he has pushed himself through as far as he can manage, reaching out with one grabbing hand.

Seems a bit strange? To make the doorway too small. Unless he wasn't always that big. I consider the bloody palm prints, and bits nailed to the wall. Unless he ate himself that big?

I urge Jackson on and channel as much energy as I can muster.

Anastassia is keeping her distance, but reaches out and cleanly slices off those clutching fingers with her blade, which immediately pop back into place like someone blowing into a rubber glove.

Anastassia has had enough and draws back her bionic arm and punches the window, which yields in an explosion of glittering fragments, and the three of us fall into the street. Meanwhile, the clown has extricated himself and disappeared to hunt down the others.

It looks like Nyx was right about Her limitations, as it would appear the clown has no jurisdiction over us out with the confines of the building.

That's a big weight off my mind!

The next room to our left contains Kal, Maddie, Nyx and Big K, the interior just as tastefully decorated as the one we've just exited.

The clown this time is pulling chunks of plaster and stone aside as he attempts to widen the doorway, while Kal launches an attack on the window.

I can see Maddie has attempted to freeze him to

stone, but she spots me through the pane and shrugs —
no go — maybe he's full of stuffing? Bullets didn't
seem to stop him anyway.

Cracks appear in the distressed glass as Kal batters
it relentlessly, and I get the feeling that even her sword
skills may not be sufficient to put this comedian down.

Nyx thrusts a single smoky arm through the glass
as Anastassia steps up and prepares to punch out the
pane. But with a twist she pulls back hard, creating a
ragged hole in the glass. I pull Jackson away as Kal
finishes the job and the dislodged shards cascade into
the street.

The clown looks appropriately angered at having
being foiled yet again and he dashes off to try his luck
elsewhere.

As the others had chosen a doorway on the opposite
side of the corridor to us, we hurry around to the front
of the building. We're just approaching the far corner
when they make an appearance.

Sophia told me that she cut her way through the
glass, with her sword, and everybody was exiting just as
the clown made his appearance, his momentum carrying
him through the doorway, taking much of the
surrounding framework with him. It sounds like
someone was getting frustrated.

Then she told me he stood at the window. 'Pulling
the ghastliest faces and making lewd gestures.' She
seemed quite disgusted by the whole display and she

thrust her flaming sword through the aperture she had just fashioned, straight into his obese stomach, and he popped! Couldn't grasp this myself when she told me, but the others confirmed it.

'Like a balloon, man!' Mel confirmed. 'There were even bits o' streamer and glitter, ye ken.'

Well, we were here, or almost, gathered on the periphery of a large plaza, at the very centre of which stood the tower in all its abhorrent glory.

Even at this distance, I could make out its shimmering surface, as if in constant flux or as if something was flowing down its exterior. And at the summit of this tower lay our persecutor and tormentor. But due to the sheer height of the monument, any details of Her remained hidden from view at this angle.

And it was really tall — heights! First a clown and then this; it's as if She's plucking my fears straight from my mind. Perhaps that's exactly what She is doing? In which case, who has a fear of biting hands? I found out a few details later about some of the phobias of the others. When I asked Mel, he said: 'Och, me? Well, I wisnae very keen on the dark when I was a bairn.' Jackson claimed to have faced his fears when he had attempted to take his life. And it turns out Anastassia was the one who had a thing about gloves; or, to be more precise, putting her hands in gloves. Who even knew that was a thing? Chirophobia was the closest thing I could come up with — fear of hands.

'How do we reach the top?' Anastassia asked of no-one in particular, as even from here it looked as if there was no obvious way to ascend.

'I guess we'll find out when we get there,' Jackson responded. 'I imagine She won't miss an opportunity to confront us face to face.'

'If She lets us get that far.'

Sanchez was right: it was still quite an expanse to cover over open ground to reach the base of the pillar.

Nyx was anxious to keep moving and we strung out behind her. Out of my team, only myself and Jackson retained a handgun each. I'd discarded my empty one back in the room with the ghastly water feature. Big K and Mel still had a pair of sidearms each: big chrome things that looked like they'd pack a punch.

I unholstered my other gun and handed it over to Anastassia, who refused. 'You may need it yet. Besides, I have this.' She flaunted that big knife, the blade's brilliance now dulled with blood and matter.

'And this.' Mist held up her axe.

Okay then, so Mist was watching out for her new buddy: cool.

Sanchez, however, graciously accepted Jackson's offer, sheathing her sticky blade.

Maddie was now solely reliant upon her keen sight; but, like me, the vicious recoil sent much of her spent ammunition well off the mark, so it wasn't especially missed. We were all very vigilant, as this would be Her final opportunity to thin our numbers further before we confronted Her. And I'm sure I wasn't the only one who doubted She would pass such an opportunity by.

The distance we had to traverse turned out to be farther than it had first appeared, and the ground before us seemed to stretch out and distort before us. It was probably far less, but it had seemed to me that we'd been walking for ages, and when I checked behind me it did seem as if we had covered a considerable distance. But when I looked ahead, it still looked as if we had at least the same distance to cover. It was like we were walking a conveyor belt, and never really making any significant progress.

'She is altering our perceptions, allowing Herself time to recover,' Sophia confirmed. 'We should prepare ourselves. I suggest we make our final stand here,' she advised.

This, as you can imagine, was met with a loud expletive from Big K. But we complied and formed a defensive circle. Who I am to ignore the advice of an angel?

Mel retrieved his second pistol and handed it to Maddie. 'Here, it disnae seem right you stondin' there wi' nae weapon.'

She nodded her gratitude at his consideration, accepting the chromed gun.

'Both hawnds.' Mel demonstrated. 'It's go' a kick like Ally McCoist.'

Maddie looked mildly bemused, as far as I could fathom with her shades on. And I'm not sure how much of that she managed to translate. And who the hell is Ally McCoist? I'm guessing a footballer? Got to be.

Anyway, she mimicked his demonstration. 'I hope this Ally McCoist is a mighty warrior?' she challenged.

'Och, the best there is.'

That seemed to mollify her at least.

Now, this was the worst part: the waiting.

The plaza was paved entirely with massive granite slabs. Quite tasteful, considering the rest of this place. Maybe She reserved the best for Her residential sphere, but contracted the rest of the decorating assignments to lesser parties? Or, on a more serious note, perhaps Her influence was considerably weaker beyond this paved area, which was a bit concerning.

The stone itself was golden and heavily flecked with silver and red. They would look quite nice in my bathroom if they were available in a smaller, more manageable size. These individual slabs must have weighed at least a ton, probably closer to two.

Jackson dipped his head in an attempt to try to catch my eye, wondering what was fascinating me. But this wasn't the time or place for divulging design concepts. So, I gave him a smile and a hand squeeze, which quelled any concerns he was nurturing.

Everyone was stoic and steadfast, except Big K, who I could see twitching and fidgeting off to my right.

Just as I was half-convinced we had stopped for nothing and that we should just continue on foot, something burst through the slabs, punching a hole clean through and devouring Sanchez whole before withdrawing. It all happened so fast no-one had time to react. I can't even tell you what it was. Sanchez didn't even have time to cry out. The creature had burrowed beneath us before striking upwards and circumventing the shield I had instantly cast as soon as we'd decided to make a stand.

'Sanchez! Jesus! Sanchez!' Big K threw himself at the hole, shouting into the depths as if this would call her back into being.

It was Mel who stepped in and grabbed him by the collar, hauling him back. 'That beastie might still be lurkin' doon there.'

That got him scrabbling back to his feet.

I inwardly chastised myself for not shielding us in all directions. It was a stupid, rookie mistake. I conjured up the image of a sphere this time, blocking any further subterranean attacks. I hoped. But that loss was going to haunt me; it was on me. But I'd have to finish beating myself up later, as that swift assault had heralded the commencement of Her next phase. And I've got to say, She's got quite an imagination.

Spherical and tar-like, with numerous protruding spinal columns rising above the glutinous mess like breaching sea serpents.

They rolled into place at a breathtaking speed from the streets at the far edge of the plaza, then came to a dead halt a short distance away, completely encircling us, smoking, boiling spoor in the wake of each, emphasising their acidic toxicity.

Note to self: avoid contact at all costs. Not that that was an option anyway, but still, it's good to underline certain things and highlight them with a bright pink fluorescent felt-pen.

Unsurprisingly, it's Big K who loses his cool first. And I quickly open a hole in our defence as I anticipate his action, as I don't fancy the idea of bullets ricocheting around the interior of the dome. I wince at the thunderous report from that shiny gun. Then he throws the spent weapon at the creature in frustration. It doesn't even flinch.

We wait a few seconds and still no movement. This is a real Mexican stand-off. I bet even Clint Eastwood with his Magnum would be scratching his head in consternation now — what do you think, punk, still fancy your chances?

What the hell were they waiting for?

An idea suddenly blooms in my head. Jackson's cottoned on and he winks at me. This would have to be quick, though, because it would mean dropping our defences.

I shift the sphere, reducing it in size as I do so, and surround the one opposite us. Jackson aids me with his telekinetic power, and together we reduce that sphere to the size of a ping-pong ball, before quickly pulling back and enforcing our protection again.

We're quick; the creatures rock on their bases and they still their progress, barely gaining a few inches when they sensed our defences were lowered. We can even hear the crushed member of their brethren bounce on the stone like a marble before rolling to a standstill — result!

On the downside, we've reached a bit of a predicament. To crush those things means dropping our guard, and I don't think they'll suppress their actions next time. Because, despite the lack of obvious sensory organs, I get the feeling they're still very aware and that they're going to be braced for a similar attack.

'Could you open a window?' Sophia asks me.

'Sure, no problem.' Maybe I'm getting a bit too cocky? But I comply; I see what she has in mind now.

I open a small hole within the sphere we inhabit, enough to allow her to direct a stream of bright energy with her sword through the aperture, and she scores a direct hit. The creature glows brightly for a few seconds like a lump of hot coal, before exploding in a shower of glowing sticky fragments.

'All right, now that's what I'm talking about!'

'I am glad you enjoy my work so much,' she comments.

But I think the sarcasm is lost on Big K, and we still

have eight to dispatch.

'We will not gain the opportunity to eliminate any two with the same method.'

Nyx confirms what I'm already thinking. This is just some bizarre game to Her, but not the kind you want to play at Christmas with the family. Well, maybe, that depends on your family.

'She is baiting us,' Kal adds. 'Forcing us to show our hand and reveal our full capabilities and ingenuity.'

Okay then, time to get creative.

Of course, we allowed Sophia a second attempt — nothing ventured... but for all the good it did, we would be as well shining a torch at it. Then came Maddie, the only other one of us, apart from myself and Jackson, who had a realistic shot at taking another one out.

I open a window for her and she steps up, raising those glasses ever so slightly. We stared on in fascination as that creature's black hide turned slowly stone grey, the colour spreading like ink through damp blotting paper.

'It's up to us now,' I inform my partner in crime. This was turning out to be one hell of a date.

'Hold up,' Mel interrupts, brandishing his gun. 'Custom-made explosive shells, worth a go, wouldn't ya reckon?'

I wave him on, keeping the window open, and he positions himself, as if at a firing range, and empties that clip.

The small charges blow fist-sized chunks out of that carcass and shards of yellow bone spin into the air. Whether it was the miniature detonations or the severing of a couple of those spinal columns, it seemed to prove successful anyway, and the creature deflates slightly as if in defeat, punctuated with a shudder, and then remains still.

Jackson took over and utilised his telekinesis to levitate one to a great height, before letting it plummet. It hit the hard stone with a sickening splat and split wide open, giving us all a glimpse of what was housed inside. Teeth at least a foot long, the kind you'd find in deep-sea angler fish. It left little room in there for anything else.

Next, he removed a large piece of that broken slab while I opened up a skylight to allow it access. Then he manoeuvred it directly above another and forced the heavy stone down to crush it.

It was beginning to creep me out now how the others just sat there, motionless, waiting for their inevitable dispatch. Unless we tried the same strategy a second time. The second slab Jackson positioned and dropped resulted in the thing skittering to the side.

Rules are rules, no repeats!

Jackson was punishing himself now — I could feel the strain as he caught up another in a kind of psychic slingshot and spun it around, before allowing the centrifugal force to carry it into the distance. The impact must have gravely damaged it sufficiently enough, because it never returned to its post.

Three to go.

I've got an idea. I project a flat disc this time right inside one, bisecting it, and the two halves fall apart, giving us a spectacle even a coroner would struggle to find fascinating without losing his lunch.

Okay, Jackson and I are on fire; we're increasing our capabilities and I'm unearthing skills I wasn't even aware I was capable of.

I turn to look at him and he knows what I've got in mind instantly. The best way I can relate it is like cocooning his energy and carrying it to our next target so it didn't diminish over the short distance. Once there, I completely encased it, while Jackson essentially vibrated it to death. Bits liquefying and exposed bone-shattering.

One left and I'm exhausted. Jackson is virtually holding me up, but he's fairing little better. His face is streaked with perspiration, cutting tracks through the monster gunk still clinging to his features.

'It's leaving,' Mist points out.

And she's right, there's no doubt about it. It's off, leaving a smoking trail in its wake.

Strange; maybe it still maintains some sense of self and therefore self-preservation? But why wait until now to leave? Wouldn't it have occurred to the others to save themselves? Or, perhaps She's weakening and this is a sign of retreat for recuperation purposes?

Either way, for now I'm grateful, and I dissolve the shield. That took it out of me; I haven't had a magic work out like that since… ever.

'A most impressive application of your talents,' Nyx praises us.

I couldn't help but give a small embarrassed smile; coming from Nyx, that means a lot.

But, her congratulations delivered, she's off, and the rest of us have no option but to tag along.

We reach the column in what appeared to be no time at all, without further molestation.

While I take a much-needed seat, Jackson at my side, Maddie and Nyx pace the perimeter in a clockwise direction, while Mist and Kal go in an anti-clockwise direction.

Sophia takes to the air to make sure our target is indeed in residence above. Any details we could gather at this stage could be beneficial to us when it came to opposing Her.

The rest of us take a moment to examine the pillar in more detail. The flux in its surface turns out to be dark liquid, virtually black, being pumped up and down the myriad of designs, glyphs and cartouches painstakingly carved into its immense surface. All of which are connected, resembling those intricate lines you find inscribed on computer circuit boards, and probably serving the same purpose: to channel energy and information. The circuit flowing both ways, allowing Her to transmit instructions and simultaneously receive and analyse information.

Sophia touches down again as the other four return from their examination of the foundations.

'No way in — it's a sealed unit,' Kal informs us, then looks to Sophia for confirmation regarding her sortie.

'It is Her.' She didn't elaborate; she didn't need to.

'Then how the hell are we going to get up there?' Anastassia cranes her neck in an attempt to see the summit.

'You want to go up there?' Big K asks, incredulous.

He's back, all neck and no spine. He looks to me and Jackson. I know what he's thinking and I shake my head. We're both seriously depleted and any energy we still do have available would be better conserved for the final confrontation. And air-lifting us all up on a psychic platform isn't viable. One slip in concentration, or "sorry, our batteries just ran out", and splat.

Sophia, likewise, can't productively utilise her power of flight. She would only be capable of elevating us one by one, to be summarily executed by Her while she returned to carry another of our team up.

It was Nyx who stepped up; it's almost as if she had been preparing herself for this moment, knowing that it was the only way.

'I will find us a way in. But regardless of what may

occur, whatever you may see, do not lose faith. Our strength is in unity.'

And with that cryptic message delivered, she phased into her shadow self and proceeded to scale the column, looking like dense diesel exhaust fumes rising across the surface. Now and again, you'd catch a glimpse of a hand or foot, but in a short time the distance reduced her to a dark smudge.

Several minutes later, Sophia took to the wing, aiming to time her arrival with Nyx. We'd made our move — I just hoped they would find a way to allow us entry to that place, too, because I doubted just the two of them would succeed; it would take all eight of us. Eight of us, there's a thing? What of Ix?

'Couldn't she have flown one of us up there?'

'I could call her back. I'm sure she would oblige in ferrying you up,' Maddie remarks to Big K playfully.

That shut him up.

And the obvious option of a portal hop was out of the question, too. Despite my exhaustion, I gave a little experimental try, but the power She was emanating up there caused the exit to warp and bend. So, I'm pretty sure we wouldn't have arrived intact. We'd just have to be patient for a little while longer.

I had full confidence in the rest of my crew as, unlike myself and Jackson, they had existed in one unbroken linear lifetime. The power they have therefore accumulated is beyond conception. Their knowledge is vast; but for the rest of us, it's hard to skip lives and still maintain knowledge. I've succeeded pretty well over the last two or three centuries, but beyond that it's like a badly remembered dream.

You can read a book in one lifetime. Then you start again, a new life. Although the essential, intrinsic knowledge of that book remains within you (as long as it's relevant to your spiritual development — I've discovered that over time), the memory of reading that book is gone.

It's a rather frustrating system, as you can imagine. The curse of mortality. But then who wants to live forever? Forever's a long time; imagine how many repeats you'd end up watching on television. It's a great show, but I can only watch the whole *Friends* boxset so many times!

'It's coming back!'

That's no way to address Sophia, and I turn to face Big K, ready to admonish him for slighting my friend. Then I realise what he's referring to. That tarry ball is hightailing back. It must be on a vengeance trip for us dispatching its brethren.

'Better regroup, then.' Jackson sighs and pulls me to my feet. There's still so much dried gore and blood coating us, I think we may very well be welded together. Our hands are going to need prising apart after this.

I got an image of a hot shower softening that gunk enough to release us then, but I'm not sharing any more of that with you!

We form a line, ever hopeful that Nyx and Sophia will come up trumps and find a way to let us in before it arrives. But they're going to have to get a move on.

I try to put up a shield, but it wavers like a curtain in a breeze, before collapsing.

'I think it's being too close to the pillar,' Jackson concludes.

You know, I think he's onto something there.

Blades are brandished, handguns aimed. This time they've got to stop it before it reaches any of us, if the melted granite at its rear is anything to go by. Skin and bone are going to be no challenge at all.

Shots are fired, then a frantic clicking: Big K's out. Maddie fires off shot after shot, but it's still coming, and she throws down the empty gun in disgust. Mel snaps his final clip in place.

Big K panics and makes a bolt for it.

'Stay in line, soldier! Stay in formation!' Anastassia bellows at him.

'Fuck that!' is his succinct response.

As it turns out, his loss of bottle could be our possible salvation as he makes for the corner of the pillar. The creature tumbles after him, possibly attracted by the movement, or just picking off a solitary opponent.

It streams past the rest of us, ignoring us for now. I'm quite sure it will be back for dessert; it looks as if it's got a big appetite.

Kal is the first to give chase, no fear whatsoever, all six blades poised for attack. This would make one hell of a video to show her self-defence class students.

Mist is close on her heels, battle-axe held high.

The rest follow on, but we're pretty much powerless at present. We make it to the corner in time to witness that ball open up to show off those incredible teeth, and I'm sure I can see something writhing in that maw as well, like a sea anemone — I watch a lot of nature documentaries.

All this takes place in just three or four seconds as it looms over Big K, who at this precise moment peers over his shoulder, cartoon-like terror painted on his face. Eyes bulging, mouth agape, arms stretched out before him like a bandage-wrapped mummy.

The anemone-like fronds extend and grasp and retract. Then those teeth snap closed in a spray of crimson and the tarry flesh flows back into place and the creature continues to roll on without losing momentum.

If I'd have witnessed the scene in a horror movie in the comfort of my own home, wrapped in a cosy blanket and eating popcorn, I would have been in hysterics; but I wasn't laughing. All that was left was a boot, and I just knew there was a foot still in there.

The creature isn't finished yet, as it takes a wide sweeping arc and heads on back. But Kal is prepared; she's waiting for it. She's already waved Mist back; this one is hers.

She's sheathed all but her demon-slayers: two four-foot double-edged blades, forged by some master smith. I kind of spoiled the moment there, sorry, but the name is long and hard to pronounce, and I always get it wrong anyway. Needless to say, he was the top man — could've been a woman actually, it never occurred to me before.

The creature aims for her; neither is backing down. Just before collision, she dives forward and plants the tips of those blades into the stone, then thrusts upwards and somersaults up and over the beast. The two swords slice deep, before she then utilises her blades again to push herself out of danger from that smoking trail.

The creature trundles on for a short while, but it runs out of steam and it eventually grinds to a halt. It's finished, and so is Big K. The thought of him inside that thing makes me shudder, and I turn away.

But what a performance from Kal — ten points from me!

'We've got our way up,' Maddie announces.

While our attention was transfixed elsewhere, a dark recess had appeared at the base of the column, like an elevator, but the kind of elevator that encourages you to take the stairs. But there are no stairs. Does this mean Nyx and Sophia were successful? Or is it, in fact, worst-case scenario, and now She has dealt with two of my friends, She's inviting the rest of us up to play?

Well, what option do we have? We enter the recess.

Coming up?

16

It was a tight squeeze, made all the more claustrophobic by the complete absence of light when the pillar sealed itself and didn't just crush us flat. That thought just occurred to me as the opening disappeared. But She must be looking forward to demonstrating Her powers before slaying us, and so keeping us alive, for now, was a fundamental part of Her plan. It was quite obvious we were playing right into Her hands. I just hoped something would occur to me, or any of us, when we finally arrived. It felt like we were travelling through something living, like moving through a digestive tract as the monster that swallowed us attempts to regurgitate us back into the light; it was most unpleasant.

I suddenly remember the thin pen-torch attached to my pistol that I have all but forgotten about, and just as I reach to retrieve it and light up all our grim faces, we reach our floor.

The stygian darkness that surrounds us simply dissipates to reveal a rather complicated scenario.

Firstly, the main event: Her, whoever She was, lay reclining in mid-air several metres above the platform, pierced with numerous tubes, cables, pipes and wires.

In fact, very little of Her body was left unravaged. Those connections linked her to the platform itself; like umbilicals, merging seamlessly with the construct upon which we were gathered. Liquids could be seen continuously pumping through the more translucent attachments, in both directions. Others pulsed with a disturbing rhythm as the fluids were channelled.

She was large, as in tall, a giant, in fact, and ancient. Not withered old — I'm one hundred-and-one-years young kind of old — but a timeless, ageless kind of old. If that makes any sense?

She was completely naked, Her visible flesh alabaster white, as was Her hair, which hung from Her scalp like a sheet. Her eyes were closed as if in sleep, appearing to be very much at peace in Her apparent dormancy, but I could sense She was very much fully aware.

Sophia was suspended off to our left, just beyond the ledge of the monument, her wings folded away, her sword sheathed. This didn't instil much confidence in me, and I could see she was suffering much pain as well.

Ix, the reason for her long absence revealed, was still encased within that transparent membrane which she had been whisked away in. Her physical form was twitching and fading in and out of focus as, I presumed, she attempted to escape her confines.

Jackson immediately ran over, dragging me with him, and placed a concerned hand on the surface of the cocoon. Ix mirrored his action. At least she was still aware and acknowledging our presence.

'She is fine… for now. The treacherous bitch.'

The voice was deep with a slight sibilant echo. As if two people were talking simultaneously, but slightly out of synch. The reason for this became clear as Nyx made an appearance from behind the thick array of tubes and pipes. Straight away, I pulled Jackson back to regroup with the others. Something was most definitely wrong with her.

'I gave her the freedom to roam my world, and this is how she repays me, by rallying dissension against me. The ungrateful whore.'

Steady on there. Someone's not happy. The rest of the team remain fixated on what's playing out, studying the scenario that's unfolding, and, I hope, formulating some sort of plan of action.

'How touching,' She laughs, indicating mine and Jackson's clutched hands. But there is no mirth in the sound. 'And I see some of the mortals who attended you on this fool's errand have survived my little dalliances.'

Wow, She called those creatures "dalliances". Loves her work, this one.

'How disappointing; perhaps if you hadn't been guided quite so successfully through the fields of the dead?' She slammed a dark fist hard against Ix's cocoon, punctuating her displeasure. 'Then I'm quite sure your numbers would have been thinned more adequately.'

She pauses here and sways as Her eyes roll over white, a small smile on Her lips, like a junkie savouring a hit.

Jackson and I glance at each other. What do we do? Jackson winks: he's got something.

Nyx, or whoever is possessing her, returns to the present and continues to prowl.

'Who are you?' Mist has found her voice and asked what I am dying to know.

That was brave of her. I'm not sure I would have wanted to draw Her attention after seeing how She's so easily controlling Nyx.

'My names are many; most are now forgotten. Some, though, still hold some significance for me: Rea; Hera; Asherah. But they are still just words, meaningless words. What is of importance is what I am. I am all!'

Oops! Someone's rattled Her cage. This woman is certifiable.

'Well screwed up in the heid, that's what you are.'

No, no, no, don't antagonise her further, Mel. But bravo all the same.

She chuckles, a deep and throaty sound; it chills me.

'Perhaps? And what of you, mortal? Do you care to taste my madness?'

She reaches out an arm, extending one finger as She

closes the gap between Herself and Mel, who takes a step back in response.

Nyx's face then suddenly contorts with concentration as she fights for control of her body, and withdraws the arm. But the effort to process and perform such an act is draining her.

'This one is strong; she still duels with me. But I like a challenge, and she will capitulate to my will. But you are not what you once were, Nyx. A shadow of your former self.' The chuckle again. 'Perhaps I will take this form permanently. I rather like it in here; it has hidden depths and untapped powers. Yes, a new body, a fresh start. I could unleash my creations into the world and finally be free of this place and rule all of Gaia, Queen of all I survey.'

Yeah, right, like that wasn't Her plan all along… and Gaia? She's showing Her age now.

Jackson nudges me and I look at him with a sideways glance while She's still preoccupied with Her visions of grandeur. The information he's harbouring slips between us and I understand immediately. His psychic abilities allowed him to connect with Nyx, however briefly, and she's still very much in the game. I get the feeling that all this is very much part of the plan.

I ever so slightly reach for the pistol Anastassia refused earlier; thank the goddess for that, or rather Anastassia.

She's still ranting.

'So much fresh, raw materials for me to utilise and experiment with.'

Wow! She's talking about people now. Doctor Frankenstein's got nothing on Her! Just keep ranting, bitch, I'm almost there.

'They will all soon know what it means to truly suffer as I proclaim an eternity of pain on them all.' She claps her hands together with unadulterated joy at the sheer thought of all that misery and pain. Her eyes close in ecstatic fantasy.

The team tense and I instigate our opening gambit. It's the best and possibly only opportunity we're going to get.

I bring my gun to bear and aim it at the myriad of connective tubes. The dense clusters mean that even with my poor aim I can't miss, and I keep pulling that trigger until I'm out. The few rounds left in the other weapon still maintained by Mel is also emptied as he follows my lead.

The bullets tear through the tangle of pipes, releasing reeking liquids and gases. Some of the smaller tubes are completely severed and the ragged edges writhe like wounded snakes, spurting blood.

The shock of this unexpected assault weakens Her hold over Nyx momentarily and she slips into her shadow form, dispersing almost completely, before then reshaping herself and disappearing into one of the larger damaged pipes.

The rest of the team take full advantage.

I notice Sophia drop from view like a stone and I hold my breath until she swoops back into view, sword held aloft. She sends in swathes of divine light, severing multitudes of connections, as Kal goes at them like a dervish.

Mist chops cleanly through the larger pipes as Jackson and I rip them apart with the combined power of our minds. Even the others rush in and start slicing with their knives.

The capsule that has held Ix captive has also dissolved, and she collapses to her knees, before forcing herself to stand and join the affray, finally receiving some recompense for the years she has been held against her will by this madwoman.

We're nearly there; despite the hundreds, possibly thousands of connections, our determination is great. We are splattered with yet more gore. No surprises there; I'm already well and truly lathered anyway, and the floor beneath our feet is slick with a pungent ichor.

At last, it's done. But what now?

Kal steps up, preparing to deliver a killing blow, but the old girl isn't done yet.

She moves quickly as She sits up in mid-air and slams Her bare feet into the muck that surrounds us, sweeping both Kal's demon-slayers aside in one swift action. The blades still cut deep into Her flesh, but no blood pours from the wounds.

That strike should've taken Her hand off!

She stands tall and Her eyes open; those orbs are zombie white. She's fully back in Her own body now. But where did Nyx go?

She sweeps Her arm across a second time and we scatter to avoid that pillar of flesh.

Mist takes advantage of the lack of cohesion the slick floor covering offers and slides low between Her legs, chopping at both Her ankles.

She howls in anguish and lashes out at Anastassia as she bravely rushes forward in an attempt to stick that blade in Her. The impact sends her flying beyond the confines of the platform, but Sophia is quick and she swoops to her rescue and carries her back to safety. She's clutching her side, though; I think she may have sustained a couple of fractured ribs.

I attempt to clamp Her arms tight against Her body with Jackson's aid. Oh, my goddess! She's strong. It's like trying to push a tree over with your bare hands. Not that I've tried, but I imagine it would be quite similar.

Kal and Mist take advantage of the temporary restrictions we've placed upon Her and chop, slash and stab unceasingly in an attempt to bring Her down.

Her now bloodless flesh hangs in strips, large chunks are cut free to reveal the snow-white musculature beneath, but still, She won't go down.

Maddie and the others can only stand by and watch

the seemingly futile onslaught, and Jackson and I certainly won't be able to keep Her arms pinned for much longer. I'm already feeling light-headed.

Suddenly, she clutches Her head, the pain She's feeling overcoming Her bondage, and She breaks free. Something's happening; it's Nyx, I just know it. She takes a couple of steadying paces back, and that's when Ix makes her move.

She's fighting Nyx every inch of the way. But Nyx is powerful and she keeps Her occupied, while Ix climbs Her massive frame; her spontaneity and speed astound me.

She reminds me of one of those mountaineers that scale cliff overhangs with no safety ropes. Just gripping on with their fingertips and a dash of chalk powder. Well, imagine that but in fast forward, and She stands between twenty-five and thirty feet in height. Ix reaches Her head in seconds and places both her hands firmly against Her temples. The goddess then simply stops — it was as if someone had just removed Her batteries or unplugged Her from the mains.

The strain of it all has finally caught up with me, and Jackson catches me before I fall. But I'm fighting that unconsciousness knocking at the door; I want to see this through to the end.

Her whole body has slumped and Her eyelids flutter as She fights to regain control. But I then notice a small flickering half-smile on Her bloodless lips. I'd recognise that smile anywhere.

We all retreat, Sophia amongst us, her illumination having little effect. She simply repelled Sophia's light. And we watch on as Nyx forces the giantess to take slow somnambulant steps towards the precipice, Ix still hanging grimly in position.

Ix explained to me later that she was shutting down certain areas of Her brain, slowly killing Her, allowing Nyx to take control of Her physical functions more easily. She can do that, Ix, remove the life-force from a living being. Although she takes no pleasure from such an act, on occasion when a living soul is suffering, then she can make that decision and end their suffering.

Anyway, back to the climactic end.

I was counting off Her ponderous steps now as She neared the edge. I was up to four; I reckoned two more would do it. She had a massive stride.

Her toes are dangling over the edge now — just one more. She knows what's coming and She hesitates, fighting Nyx and Ix every inch of the way — they sound like two pixies, don't they? Sorry, totally out of context — this is a serious moment. But, finally, that last step is extracted and She steps into the air and slowly topples forward as Her centre of gravity takes over.

Ix scrambles over Her head as it pitches forward and down Her back, before launching herself for the platform's edge. Her body "ghosts" — it's the description that best relates to you what happens. Her physical form fades and becomes ethereal, her skull becoming more prominent during the process. She breaches the seemingly impossible distance to land effortlessly, knees bent, arms slightly extended to balance her landing. Only then does she solidify again, her ghostly pale skin darkening to that chocolate brown hue once more.

How is it everyone's got a cool superhero landing except me? I wonder how agile Jackson is?

Stop it, Alice! This is serious.

I'm focusing again and already I'm concerned about whether or not that fall will actually kill Her? It is a long way down, but still? And where's Nyx?

There's an ominous rumble that feels like an earthquake, and it slowly builds in intensity. We have to leave now before this tower disintegrates. The fall must have killed Her after all, I conclude, as the tower sways and a sizeable chunk of stone breaks off the side. With Her gone, there's nothing left to cohere this place.

'She is gone,' Ix confirms, as she rejoins us. 'You need to take control, Alice, and lead us from here.'

'I don't know if... How do I...?' I'm mumbling now — pull yourself together, Alice. And how did she know my name? Jackson must have told her. I give myself a mental slap on the head.

I indicate that we should join hands and I'm mightily relieved as a dark, shifting form oozes onto the platform, and seconds later Nyx is solidifying at my side and takes my hand.

'I made my exit once Her demise was assured. Her mind was a cesspit of corruption.' She pulls a small face in disgust.

'You knew Her, didn't you? Did you always suspect it was Her?'

'I had my suspicions. And yes, I knew her once, many, many centuries ago when She was... different. But the power She wielded corrupted Her beyond redemption. There was no hope of salvation for Her.'

Nyx looks sad at Her passing. Another fallen titan; there are so few left now, if at all.

'We should be leaving!' Mist breaks my little reverie.

The vibrations increase and large shards peel away from the sides of the pillar. Our circle is complete and I close my eyes.

I visualise my cabin in the forest; the lake, with its crystal-clear waters; the stone bear outback; the cicadas chirruping at dusk; the scent of rich musty loam and the tangy odour of pine. And I mean I can *really* smell that pine, almost taste it.

Wait a...

'You can open your eyes now,' Jackson whispers.

I did it! Totally awesome, we're back home. The air is so fresh, I'd almost forgotten. I take a deep lungful and savour the taste.

Ix is staring around in wonderment. This must be

her first excursion out of that place, the first time she's smelled fresh air in centuries.

Anastassia and Mist are hugging — saw that one coming — but gently, as Anastassia's in some pain. Turns out she sustained three broken ribs as a direct result of that impact, and a monster bruise that took several weeks to fade.

Kal is beaming at me, filled with pride at my accomplishment. I think I'm blushing under my monster gunk facepack.

Sophia's all radiant and smiley and Maddie gives me a double thumbs-up. I'm sure she picked that up from the Fonz, watching sneaky reruns of *Happy Days*. You know, I thought I'd heard strains of the theme tune when I'd gone to bed. They do have rather eclectic and bizarre tastes regarding the television, those that partake at least. I know Kal hasn't yielded to its hypnotic allure, but Mist, for example, has discovered the joys of cage fighting recently!

'Thank you and well done,' Nyx whispers to me.

'You couldna magic me up a wee dram, could ya?' Mel inquires.

And just as Jackson sweeps me into a hug, I pass out. I hope he didn't misinterpret that as a swoon?

17

That was a week ago now, more or less. Anastassia and Mel were picked up and whisked away in an unmarked military vehicle yesterday. Kal had to physically restrain Mist as the vehicle departed, despite their assurances that they would return soon. But for now, they were still part of a military operation and duty called: reports had to be made and filed.

Ix departed shortly afterwards. She had her responsibilities regarding the newly dead, or certain factions at least. She had to oversee the restoration of pathways and gateways and guide them on their way. Once the system was flowing satisfactorily again, she would return.

But she certainly enjoyed and made the most of her new-found freedom, spending much of her time wandering the pristine forest and absorbing all the life that thrived there. Not like some kind of energy-sucking amoeba, but just in an appreciative, metaphorical sense. It had been so exhilarating after being surrounded by so much death, she said. She had even lost that gaunt, undernourished look, too. I wouldn't go so far as to say that she was exactly healthy-looking — rosy-cheeked isn't an expression I would use when describing Ix. How healthy can someone look with a skull face anyway? But she emanated life, and for someone who had been submerged in death for so long, that was an immense achievement.

I walked with her a little way before she departed, watching as she faded away like a ghost. I was sorry to see her go. We'd become a small tight-knit community over such a short period due to our unique ordeal, so it was hard to say goodbye, however temporarily.

Jackson, despite his military ties, stayed on.

Big smiley emoji!

As he said, he wasn't military personnel, so they had no jurisdiction over him — and they could shove their protocol. He said that as well to the high-ranked officer that turned up with the full intention of escorting him, together with Anastassia and Mel, off the premises. But when confronted with a rather determined-looking crowd of goddess warriors, Kal in her blue many-limbed form, he decided it best to leave with just the two recruits.

That's almost where we are now… almost. Stick around, it's not over yet. But for now, I'll backtrack to when we first returned home. Or, to be more exact, when I first regained consciousness.

All I wanted was a long hot shower, followed by a long hot soak in the bath. There was no way I was lying down on my freshly laundered sheets in congealed bodily fluids from indescribable monstrosities. And despite the multiple protests that I should instead sleep and recuperate, I got my own way.

Hell, this was my house!

The rest of them soon saw the benefits and allure of a good thorough cleaning and it soon led to a queue forming for the bathroom. Nyx, although not requiring the same personal hygiene requirements, pulled a sneaky one and shadow-phased through the bathroom door and secured first place.

'I didn't know you could do that?' I asked her later on.

'Neither did I.'

Seems like we're all experiencing new talents.

I even allowed the use of my en suite; unheard of before now. Mist (who threatened to chop down the bathroom door if Nyx didn't unlock it, like in *The Shining* — so I had to relent really; I was too tired to refuse), Anastassia and Jackson were granted that privilege as well. He's clean for a guy (or is that just the slobs I've encountered?) and tidy, too; extra brownie points to him!

Then I slept for a day — on my own! Well, not exactly. Jackson crashed out beside me, but we both just slept, his presence still very much a comfort to me.

I'm pretty sure everyone took the opportunity as well, even Mist the insomniac, after she and Mel found my bottle of maple whisky and demolished it. I wouldn't have drunk it anyway.

By the time I hit that soft mattress, I was too tired to even consider food. I managed a cup of chamomile and that was me. Good night, Canada!

We did very little over the next few days; we deserved a break. So, we watched movies, we ate, a lot, and shared stories. Turns out Mel's quite the comedian. Real name Derek, a former truck driver. He even lets me call him Deek now. Derek was just a stretch too far. He had us in stitches with his bluntness and Scottish way with language.

'So, then, God's wife, mad as a brush just like ma old nan afore she went knockin' on heaven's gate.'

Sophia, in all seriousness, informed him that no such construction actually existed.

'What is it, then?' he asked.

'To reach the heavenly realms, a soul must pass through many angelic realms in order to purge their sins, evolving until a true state of divinity is finally achieved.'

'Aye, well, that's ma nan fucked, then!'

You just couldn't make this stuff up.

We laughed and we cried, the release of pent-up emotion expressing itself in many ways. We mourned those we had lost. The loss of Sanchez still preyed heavily on my conscience.

I spoke to Ix about this and she assured me upon her return to the realms of the dead that she would seek out the spirits of those we had lost and personally guide them on their journey. I must admit I felt a little better after that.

Then came talk of the future and the plans and dreams each of us had. Anastassia and Deek intended on quitting the military as soon as conceivably possible. I had always thought that once signed-up, you were bound contractually to complete a certain designated number of tours of duty.

'Aye, well, we'll just see about that!' Deek obviously had other ideas.

As for his plans, he said he'll take it as it comes — very philosophical. Anastassia plans on returning here. I told her she was always more than welcome; Deek, too, come to that. But he admitted to missing city life and, 'I'd better pay ma old ma a visit.'

But for me, I had plans. I'm getting to that.

Maddie and Nyx showed a certain reluctance to return to the apartment in New York and open shop again, as did Kal regarding her classes. The experience we had all shared had certainly changed us, altered our perspectives and changed our priorities.

Mist had already made her home here — and she was just a bear with a sore head until Anastassia returned.

I had hoped Jackson would hang around; I dropped enough hints, without appearing to be too desperate and clingy. Hey, a girl can get lonely out here in the forest, and for the first time in forever, I finally felt comfortable where I was and with who I was, both physically and spiritually.

Sophia confessed that she would probably return to modelling, but admitted that she would miss us all too much to stay separated for long. I was rather surprised and touched by this sentiment. The fashion industry, as I had always suspected, she said, was populated by shallow, narcissistic fools. And the whole experience had left her feeling rather jaded, her faith in humankind draining slowly away. And she didn't want that; she wanted to see the good that she knew was inherent in people.

Now that was the perfect opportunity, I thought, to spring my cunning masterplan.

'How about we put a band together?'

Silence descended like nightfall. Perhaps not such a good idea, after all. Wait a second... Anastassia is nodding.

'That sounds cool.'

Bassist — check!

'I could sing,' Sophia chips in.

Hmm, bit disappointed — I was hoping for that slot myself. I'm jumping ahead a bit here, but we got a karaoke session going later, and it turns out that she can sing. She's got the voice of an — what else? — angel.

Singer — check!

Confession time: Kal's been secretly learning the

drums. She's a dark horse, although I don't know if she's been practising with two or six arms — now that I'd like to see!

Drummer — check!

This is looking decidedly promising.

While we're confessing, I've been a bit of a writer over the years. Oh, you figured that one out! And as a result, I've accumulated a lot of song lyrics, and, well, I think they're pretty decent. Great minds and all that, Jackson has a talent for the written word as well.

So, we've got material, too.

Deek volunteered to drive the tour bus. We're thinking well ahead now, but hey, why not?

Maddie and Nyx are already discussing merchandising opportunities. Their combined artistic talents would definitely add a certain original flair, and their accrued business acumen would undoubtedly stretch to managing the band.

That left Mist.

'We still need a lead guitar?' I dropped this one to see what the response would be.

Anastassia looked straight at her. She's thinking the same as me, and if anyone can persuade her...

'You could swap out your battle-axe for an axe?'

Go, Anastassia.

Mist didn't click at first, didn't make the connection until it was explained.

'Axe is a slang term for a guitar,' Anastassia

revealed, enlightening her.

Was that a smile I caught? I think she likes the idea. Well, that was easier than I'd anticipated. The right time, the right place, I guess. Oh, and we hadn't occluded Ix either; she was on a late-night walkabout when the subject was broached by me. By the time she returned, we were in full swing, and she has the most haunting voice that complements Sophia's own beautifully, so:

Lead guitarist — check!

Backing vocalist — check!

Caught up in the excitement, we quickly rallied together and found Mist the ideal guitar online. And no prizes for guessing that it was axe-shaped!

I didn't forget Jackson's new hat, either! There'll be a small bonfire later for the cremation of certain items of clothing. Hell! All of it — there's no way I'm wearing any of that stuff again.

The time we spent together over those few days was some of the best I'd ever experienced, and now I've more memories to cherish. So many in such a short period; mind you, it's long overdue. I'm not complaining, and here's hoping that there's many more to come.

But things are quietening down now. Mist and Anastassia are spending more time together, making the most of it before duty calls Anastassia away. Jackson and I are forging a strong bond, easier done when not in hell, and the future's looking very bright for a change.

Ix, she comes and goes, filled with delight at witnessing butterflies, hearing birds singing, the sound of gentle rain and the wind soughing through the trees. She is very child-like and innocent in many ways and takes such pleasure from simple things. She has certainly made me look at nature in a new and refreshing way.

Anyway, we're making the most of all this peace and solitude, as the construction of the new studio commences soon. At least the local trees will be used more constructively this time. More of a studio-come-guest house really, as I'm going to need the extra rooms for our growing community.

So, I'll leave you for now. Jackson's waiting for me: we're heading down to the lakeside with a picnic. You know, I can't ever remember doing that — the picnic by the lake, I mean.

So, constant companion, you may sleep easy in the knowledge that those monsters have ceased tearing their way into your world. You may have even caught a few of the stories on one of the news channels or online. Have you heard the stories about the newly discovered species previously unknown to science? All dead, thankfully. Although I'd noticed myself that there was no photographic evidence to corroborate the reports. The military saw to that, I'm sure. Our dealing with Her laid them to rest, permanently. The odd story will still leak for a short while yet, I feel, and the media will continue to debunk many as hoaxes, no doubt.

But we know better, don't we?

Interlude

I'm so glad you decided to grace me with your presence again; it really wouldn't be the same without you. I'd feel as if I was just talking to myself otherwise. Well, not *see* you as such, but you know what I mean.

It's been just over a year now since we last interacted, from my perspective at least. I know, how time flies.

It' been a busy time at my end. And great news! We did successfully form our band and pressed our first disc — I think I can use that phrase now, as vinyl has made a comeback — two months ago now.

It's charted and doing well; perhaps you've even heard it or bought a copy yourself?

Deek did return to Glasgow after being discharged from the military on PTSD grounds, but promises he'll be behind the wheel when we begin our tour. A tour! Crazy, right? It all feels like a dream. Flying between venues was considered as an option, but I felt we'd be letting Deek down — he was so excited at the prospect of driving the bus. Besides, after reconsideration — a road trip — it was a no-brainer.

Anastassia, who I'm glad to inform you fully

recovered from her injuries, was also discharged after being diagnosed with PTSD. (I think the two of them played the system a bit to obtain that diagnosis. But who could blame them!) I have to admit, though, I've been a bit paranoid about masked Navy SEALs infiltrating the area and kidnapping us. Anastassia assures me, though, that she kept details regarding the specifics of our covert mission to a bare minimum, which included details about the rest of us. But I strengthened my network of magic trip wires and installed a few more just to be safe.

Jackson also made a few calls; turns out he's quite well connected, got a lot of friends in high places (I won't mention any names here) who have made certain promises regarding our continued anonymity and privacy. Despite certain assurances, he did subtly let them know that any military incursion on my property or harassment against himself or his friends would be considered an infringement of our civil rights and would be met with an aggressive response. So, I think the fact that we successfully transmitted ourselves, then returned from the underworld after expediting hordes of unnameable creatures, went a long way towards the powers-that-be leaving us well alone.

For now, at least.

Where was I? Oh, yes. Kal, Mist and Nyx built our new studio slash guest house; once they began construction, there was no stopping them. We all mucked in actually, including Anastassia — despite her injury, she was determined not to be excluded. But those three did the bulk of the carpentry and construction work. They even took a more serious approach to forest management — so I'm not now living in the middle of a field — only felling pine trees I had marked out for the project. They had it pretty much completed in four months and we were in there practising for real a few weeks later.

Jackson's in Madingley, a small village not far from Cambridge, to tie up some loose ends, pick up some clothes and personal possessions, that kind of thing. He did make the offer for me to accompany him, and I was tempted. Being apart from him is hard, but I'd rather stay at home for now in light of recent events, just in case. If some general or other shows up, then I'd rather be here to maintain some sort of peace. Besides, I'm the only one that could whisk us all away at a moment's notice if required.

Then, when he gets back, he's officially moving in. If you could only see my big smile right now! We took things slowly, but I think it was an inevitable conclusion in the end.

Maddie and Nyx are in LA, organising tour stuff, at the moment. I leave all the details to them. Much of what they achieve, they do from the base here online, but sometimes they're required to put in an appearance. They're far more persuasive face to face when it comes to negotiating. They're driving, as well. Maddie is, anyway: stole my pick-up! Well, not stole it as such. Said they didn't have the freedom of portal casting to get around. Maddie's a good driver, though; she'll look after it, and with her mechanical talents, there's no danger of them becoming stranded on the road. Nyx, for the record, can't drive: she's terrible. But I think she quite enjoys being chauffeured everywhere.

Sophia's appearing in her final fashion show a week on Friday, and we've all promised to attend, even Deek — I said I'd pick him up. He said he wouldn't miss it for the world:

'What? All those bonnie lasses dressed to the nines in designer gear? Just try an' stop me.'

I don't know if that's quite the right attitude, but Sophia would want him there. We're a family now, warts and all.

Ix, as promised, returned about a month after she left us. In the realm of the dead, that equated to about six months, or maybe nearer a year. Funny how time bends between different planes; it's really hard to accurately compensate for that. It's not as if there are designated time zones or anything.

I'd been having recurring dreams about my sister from my previous life a couple of weeks before Ix showed up. I hadn't even thought about her much; you learn to move on with each successive new beginning. Much of what I can recall from previous lifetimes I remember as snippets, like badly remembered dreams.

But these had increased in detail and clarity recently, particularly those regarding Emily. But, strangely, I have no recollection of our parents; only that they died when I was in my early teens.

Emily took on the mantle of a parent, but sadly died of cancer several years after our parents. She was only twenty-two. I can picture her face quite clearly now, something I would have been completely unable to do last year.

My point being: these dreams were every night, sometimes two or three times. But not bad dreams; they were good memories of better times. One night, though, I just couldn't sleep, so I went out to clear my head: a midnight stroll in the forest. I do that now and again; it's quite safe out here and I remember the moon was almost full, giving everything that frosted look. That's when Ix made an appearance — just walked right out of thin air. She would be amazing on one of those *Celebrity Haunted* programmes. Just to see the looks on the presenters' faces as this ghostly floating skull manifested itself after years of filming nothing more than the occasional orb. She frightened me, anyway.

It was really good to see her, though. I hadn't realised how much, until she put in an appearance.

We walked together and talked for a long time, until dawn.

I'll relate the details, combining them with a short excursion we both made a few weeks later.

When she made me the offer of escorting me over to the other side, I was understandably wary. My previous experience was somewhat overwhelming, to say the least, but she assured me things had changed for the better. And she wasn't kidding.

The crossing was a very different experience compared to my brand of unique travel. She took my hand and we walked into another world. This realm simply faded away and we were there. It was very peaceful and smooth, the way it should be for those leaving their physical forms.

The place we entered was a vast plain of luxuriant grasses gently rippling in the warm breeze beneath sherbet skies. Small trees, of a species I've never seen before, with foliage of a shade of colour I have no words to describe, punctuated the otherwise unmarred landscape. It was idyllic and heavenly, the atmosphere one of tranquil repose. The grasses silky to the touch, the gentle breeze laced with faint traces of sweet scents that dazzled my senses.

And set within this landscape were three domineering archways, the frames of which appeared to be carved from a wood that glistened like precious metal, inlaid with numerous designs from a multitude of cultures and historical periods.

'Where are we?'

'You have trod this path before,' she smiled, waiting for me to connect the dots.

'No!' It was so transformed.

'This place is where the newly dead are conveyed before they continue on their journey.'

'But how?' I was taken aback. If you'd witnessed the before and after transformation, you'd realise why. Gone now were the endless fields of corpses and grasping hands. It was miraculous.

'Are those bodies still…?' I glanced at the ground, a little creeped out at what may still be lurking under the grasses.

'Their flesh is now a part of this place, their spirits gone.'

I don't know if she meant like compost part of this place or not? But I let that go; I didn't want to tarnish my visit here.

'Many spirits sojourn here for a time, but instinctually their soul knows what is expected and most are eager to undertake the next step.'

'Sanchez?' I hadn't forgotten her.

Ix nodded. 'Her and many others are now at peace and beginning new lives, including Emily.'

What? She knew about Emily?

'She asked after you; she said she was sorry she had to leave you at such a vulnerable age to fend for yourself.'

You'll have to bear with me, as I've blended that visit with the discussion we shared on the night Ix returned. I'm not ashamed to admit that I broke down at receiving this news. And I sat among the pines and cried as I've never cried before; it was such an emotional release.

Ix remained at my side until I had purged myself. I was rather shaky when I got to my feet. But the love I felt for Emily and for this woman who had delivered this message to me at that moment was very profound.

I have since unearthed a small image of Emily I sourced after much genealogical detective work online, which I wear always in a small locket about my neck.

And it wasn't until that private moment with Ix that I realised I had finally resolved my past lives and could take a firmer step into the future. It was my unresolved issues regarding Emily that had been unknowingly preventing me from fully living in the present.

I will always be eternally grateful to Ix for that kindness, and to Emily. I just wish I had had the opportunity to spend more time with her and appreciate more of what she sacrificed to look after me.

An angel in the truest sense of the word.

It was all very emotional, but in an amazing way. Purging my soul of guilt and regret. I highly recommend it.

Now, the matter of those three arches. They were just planted there a little distance apart from each other. The details of what lay beyond them were hard to fathom and were the same when viewed from both sides.

'One will carry the soul into a new life back on Earth. Those who are deserving of an opportunity to evolve and progress. Another draws in the dark souls amongst us. Those with no regrets for the wicked deeds they have committed, tainted souls, and those who have no belief in the continuation of the spirit. This final gateway...' — she brought me before the middle arch — 'is for souls ready for transformation. Those of us gifted with boundless compassion. This takes them beyond physical realms into the divine, celestial and angelic realms. And places yet to be discovered.'

I didn't realise we had so many options!

Profound, right? But very enlightening. I felt very privileged at being allowed this insight into the age-old imponderable of life after death. This was it, right here!

'What's to prevent souls from entering the wrong gateway?'

'When their spirits arrive, only one gateway will be visible to them, only one option available. It is pre-ordained upon their death.'

Pretty good system, right?

'What happens to those tainted souls?' I had to ask. Not out of sympathy; it was just curiosity.

'Their essence is dispersed. They simply cease to exist in this or any other realm.'

Wow! Beware, bad people and non-believers, apparently there's no going back from here. Ix continued to explain that this system had been corrupted many, many aeons ago. And now, finally, she could be at peace, as the structural system was self-sustaining.

I witnessed a single tear glistening on her cheek as she shared this with me. Not just at the freedom this now personally granted her, but the peace and security it offered the spirits of the dead.

So, dead is just a word, and death merely a transitory state. You heard it here first!

Before we left, she clasped my hand, allowing me to see. And I saw dead people (like in that film!) everywhere; well, the ghosts of dead people, of all ages, colours and creed. Sitting, standing, walking. Staring up at the beautiful sky, many more standing before the arch that beckoned to them, awaiting their soul to cross the threshold and continue the journey. For those of them who were deserving, at least.

I took the opportunity, during our private walk, to ask about my future. Jackson's and my own, to be exact. As I've mentioned before, the rest of the team are immortal and can, therefore, cross into these divine realms, Ix included; but what of us mere mortals? The thought of growing old and dying with the possibility of starting again didn't appeal. If there was a way out, I was in.

Ix explained that if my soul wasn't ready for transformation, then that gateway wouldn't have been visible to me. Good to know. I wonder if Jackson can see it? Because one day I'd like to think the two of us will step over that threshold together. With the rest of the team, too, all eight of us together; now that's an image that warms my heart.

Pretty heavy, right? But I felt compelled to share that with you, so you could understand what all of this has been in aid of — battling gods and goddesses — it's so things could be fixed for every single person on this planet, and for those yet to reincarnate.

There was much more discussed regarding deities, divine beings and the presence of hell and the existence of demons. Turns out hell doesn't exist; that's kind of reassuring, isn't it? The place we visited was simply an extension of Her warped and corrupted personality. I picked Kal's brains regarding demons and their origins, but it was a surprisingly complicated subject. Much of them coalesced from the nefarious minds of humankind, or the remnants of wicked deities. Humankind was made in God's image, but the Devil made many in his image, too, apparently. Which raises far more questions than it answers. But I'll not dwell on further details, as that isn't essentially what this story is about. Besides, there have to be some mysteries left in life, right?

Well, Ix did stay on after that and we take the time to share walks through the forest and get all philosophical. She still makes me jump with that floating skull thing, though. Don't know if I'll ever get used to that.

So, that's where we all are at present. Life's good,

and I'm still getting used to it. I'm just waiting for the next fly in the ointment. And rest assured, that fly did indeed make an appearance.

Three days ago, whilst I was writing some new lyrics down by the lakeside and the girls were taking time out to put together a bench and table — very professional it is, too — I became aware of Mist approaching from behind me.

'You should come quickly.'

I could tell immediately that she was concerned about something other than the chords to our latest track. She can play, by the way. Apparently, if it looks like an axe, then she can handle it with aplomb.

'What's going on?' I was a little bit put out; I'd been really in the zone and putting down some good lyrics. But the look in her ice-blue eyes demanded my immediate attention.

This "something" was serious.

We hurried back to the house, and I could pick up the atmosphere that emanated from there before we entered, and a feeling of foreboding clutched at me.

'The picture television screen has revealed a further development,' she added, as we skipped up the steps.

I know, that's just what she calls it. Actually, I think it's kind of cute! By now I had images of monsters stalking the streets and tearing people to shreds, a trail of devastation in their wake. I had to see this with my own eyes.

Everyone who was currently in residence was gathered around the "picture television screen", all eyes fixed to the image being broadcast.

"... *reports are coming in of what appears to be the presence of... I can't believe I'm actually about to say this, an artificial intelligence that has miraculously appeared within Stonehenge. The prehistoric stone circle located in Wiltshire, England, played host to this miraculous occurrence sometime in the early hours of this morning. One eye witness who was in the vicinity at the time states that the figure, which is estimated to stand around forty feet in height, simply materialised out of thin air. This being outwardly appears to be some form of cyborg, although experts have conjectured that the true identity of this being is yet to be revealed. And the golden effigy is possibly some form of protective suit. Already hundreds of members of the public have descended on the site, which has long been believed...*"

The reporter then droned on for a while about the circle's history and the many theories regarding its construction.

I quickly read the news stream that ran along the bottom of the screen, but gleaned little further information regarding this sinister visitor that hadn't already been disclosed.

An aerial shot transmitted from a drone showed us the full extent of the hysteria this unexpected arrival had generated, and a rather inadequate cordon had been hastily set up in an attempt to keep the amassing throng from overwhelming the site.

The dark uniforms of the police and the military could be easily discerned below as they formed an impenetrable ring of bodies around the circle and the source of the excitement itself. Many members of the public were hoisting placards above the heads of the crowd emblazoned with messages welcoming this, in their eyes, an alien visitor to our world. Hundreds more held high phones as they recorded this monumental moment for posterity.

And, of course, the main attraction — like nothing I've ever seen before, and I've seen one or two things. The drone descended, focusing on the statuesque golden figure. It, or rather she, looked like someone had crossed a *Barbie* doll with *C3-PO*. She was beautiful, totally alien, potentially very dangerous and apparently asleep.

She was just standing there, eyes shut, arms held at her sides, standing to attention. What was she? And where had she come from? And most importantly, what did she want?

We were all silently fixated on the image before us, individually pondering these questions and the implications of such a visitation, when those eyes suddenly opened.

Well, here we go again!

18

Have you been tuned in to the coverage? I'm sure you have. I mean, who isn't? This is super-colossal! I bet you weren't expecting this kind of development? I certainly wasn't, and I've come to expect the unexpected. I mean, this could well be the first genuine alien contact the human race has encountered. It puts all the decades of grainy photographs of hubcaps to shame, doesn't it?

At this point, you probably know about as much as us regarding this event. Well, almost. I'll update you as things progress. And since she "woke up", there haven't been any further developments, except for the numerous speculative explanations, many of them bizarre and outlandish.

An advertising publicity stunt for an upcoming video game — really?

That story broke four days ago now and the crowd has gathered in force; it looks like Glastonbury down there. And it looks like the whole of the British forces have been mobilised as well. But I'll bet the local town and village businesses are booming. Already merchandisers are cashing in. T-shirts are flying off the hook with rather tacky images of the golden girl, the unimaginative slogan "I come in peace" (we'll see about that) emblazoned below.

Since the breaking news, I began contacting those absent team members, transporting Maddie and Nyx — oh, it's Nikki now, by the way; I'll explain in a second — directly back to my cabin in the woods, my pick-up truck as well. They just drove it right on through. I must admit I was properly proud of myself for that one. An update on that: I don't need to spill blood to conjure a new portal any more, which is great news for me. Seems this new development became available to me since our return from that place. Or it could've been since our full quota of eight was re-established, as I never needed to injure myself when portal casting in the underworld. It just never occurred to me at the time; it just seemed so natural.

I then relocated us to my London pad; it made sense under the circumstances. Jackson soon joined us and Deek turned up yesterday — took the train down from Scotland, declaring that recent events were "pure mental, man!".

It was Deek who started referring to Nyx as Nikki, and she kind of liked it, declaring to us all that we should refer to her as Nikki from now on. Got to admit I liked it, too. Only Deek could have encouraged that.

Sophia flew in from Tokyo just a few hours ago: business class, not Seraph style. She's sleeping now;

even divinities suffer jet lag, apparently. She's so adorable when she's sleeping, like a curled-up kitten, glowing like an incandescent night light.

I forgot how much I liked this place. It's a little cramped with us all here, but the ceilings are high and the place is contemporarily decorated with a fresh, spacious feel to it. Especially since the addition of numerous pot plants, courtesy of Kal when she was living here (self-watering system in each pot, in case you wondered; ideal for when you're travelling), and I love the four-foot-high wooden Kwan Yin in the entrance hall.

Jackson's been busy on the phone, trying to get put through to someone in authority, finally managing — after resorting to the use of some choice language — to eventually get someone to take him seriously. There's so much internal restructuring constantly being implemented within those organisations, it proved hard to track down any of his previous "friends in high places".

Needless to say, weapons are primed and many military advisors are recommending an immediate missile strike. But there are just too many imponderables; enough to stay their fire, at least for now.

Have you seen *The Day the Earth Stood Still*? She just stands there, unblinking, waiting, just like the robot in that. I noticed a few of the movie channels are rerunning it.

The whole world is on pause.

As to who or what she is? Well, keep this under your hat as we haven't disclosed this information to anyone. Nyx, sorry Nikki, assures us all that she is Nephilim. And it doesn't take a genius to work out that she's waiting for us.

Now, the Nephilim, if the information available online and in print is to be relied upon, were the result of God's sons and men's daughters getting together, and loosely translated means giants. Nikki claims that they were a separate species of divine being that were elemental in the creation of many worlds, including our own. So, if she is to be believed, and I have no reason to doubt her, then this golden Nephilim was in a sense our one true God. Or at least a representative of such. Now that's going to turn religion on its head; I bet the Pope never envisioned that!

Their origins? Even Nikki couldn't enlighten us there; we just know that they're not from this world, possibly don't even originate from this galaxy.

Sophia's contact with these beings was very different to that representative that had us all glued to our television sets, remembering them as light beings, amorphous, with no fixed definition. So, our visitor's golden exterior was quite possibly some kind of survival suit, as many so-called experts had speculated.

But despite hours of brainstorming and idea

swapping, we haven't formulated any kind of concrete plan of action. But one thing's for sure, we'll have to make our move soon as there are too many loud, influential voices in the wrong places with very itchy trigger fingers right now. Which means it looks like we'll just have to comply and do what she is waiting for — visit her.

A more conventional method of arrival was first agreed upon. It made logical sense, as I didn't want to flaunt my abilities or antagonise her into responding unfavourably; or the military, for that matter. Certainly not with all that media coverage going on. We don't want the public to think that they've been invaded by aliens and the golden girl was just the spearhead and was just biding her time until reinforcements arrived.

It's been decided, then.

Jackson got straight on the phone and was put through to the prime minister no less. We get picked up at 'four of the am' — why do military types have to talk like that? They could've just said stupid o'clock. And then we'll be transported by helicopter directly to the site. It's just past 10am now, so we've got a little less than eighteen hours.

Jackson looks nervous and we grab a private moment to talk about it. And I know his concern isn't built on the presence of the Nephilim. It's the large military propinquity, and we'll be slap bang in the middle of it all.

We read each other so well, sometimes we just don't even need to speak; we just perceive what each other is feeling, what we're thinking. If it sounds a bit invasive, trust me, it has many benefits!

So, what we're both thinking is: if this first contact goes pear-shaped and the team have to go on the defensive — or worse, offensive — then this could play out as some *Marvel* box office hit. But on the flip side, it could be our saving grace as well. If we come out of this in a positive light as a result of the media coverage, then the military would be cast in a rather dubious light if they were seen to be detaining us.

Although, I wish them luck with that one!

Despite our album currently climbing up the charts — number three right now, with it expected to hit the number one spot next week — we've kept our identities secret. We were planning to reveal ourselves on tour. Deek suggested masks, but that idea got the thumbs-down. Looking back now, the suppressing of our ipseity was particularly good foresight on our part; otherwise, upon our arrival, I'm sure the millions tuned in would be clamouring to hear a few tunes. This is going to blow the lid off the cookie jar; there'll be no going back from here.

Ipseity — I thought I'd throw that one in there (I might not get another opportunity to furnish you with another word for the day) — means individual selfhood, and can also refer to the essential element of heavenly moments. I thought it uniquely expressive, considering what many of us are.

Anyway, the band's success is one thing, but global defenders of the Earth? I can't remember signing up for that!

So, myself and Jackson are very much on the same page. On the plus side, we'll probably shift a lot of records. I did hear Maddie say the publicity we could gain in respect of the upcoming tour is better than anything she and Nikki could have generated. Remember, the immortals amongst us don't see things through mortal eyes; the repercussions of our actions just don't seem to apply to them, or they don't recognise them, at least.

But if Kal goes blue and switches on her blender mode, then every general all over the world is going to sit up, take notice and ask: "Why haven't we got one of those?"

A step at a time, Alice, a step at a time.

I'm off again! Sophia! She'll be recognised by countless people when she shows up. And Mist, the infamous "manacled woman". Oh, what's the point? My brains are going to liquefy at this rate and run out of my ears, and that would ruin my hair again! I grew out the black and got my hair cut short, by the way. No matter how many shampoos I had, I was convinced that there was still monster crud in there. Jackson likes it, so that's good enough for me.

I spent a little quiet time with Ix; she's become like my guru or something. Kal's great, too, but there's something about Ix's company. Maybe it's been all that time spent with those filled with loneliness and anguish at the point of death: suicides; mothers in childbirth; individuals who die in the act of protecting others. She is the personification of compassion; she's become my rock in all this, and Jackson's, too, and as long as I'm close to him as well, I feel stronger and more confident.

Turns out my magical perception spell doesn't obscure Ix's skull face. It's to do with mortal beings always subconsciously aware of their mortality — makes sense, I guess; you can't hide from who or what you are. So, our cover story is that it's the latest in holographic tattoos. Don't know if anyone's going to buy that, but it's all I've got. I don't recall the *Avengers* having any stuff like this to contend with?

We're just waiting then, like the rest of the world. The Nephilim still hasn't moved; no surprises there. We refer to her now as Maria; it was Deek again who came up with that: 'I kent she reminded me o' summat. The lass in that black an' white movie *Metropolis*, ye ken, by that Fritz summat or other. It's a classic.'

He located a few images online for us and you know what, she does look a bit like our visitor. So, the name stuck.

But her glowing unearthly eyes, even through the medium of television, touch on something primeval deep within you; you've probably experienced the feeling yourself. You just know that beneath that golden façade lies something fiercely intelligent and very much alive.

19

Four am! Urgh! Why did we agree to this? I'm still waiting to wake up from this nightmare.

Wait, no it's real!

We're good to go. Kal has the holdall containing her various blades and Mist's indispensable axe, which I've come to realise never needs sharpening, due to its enchanted heritage. Sophia's sword is as much a part of her as her wings, only revealing itself when she fully transforms. Very handy.

There it is… I can hear our transport arriving. An entourage of jeeps that will ferry us to an abandoned airstrip on the outskirts of London somewhere.

Six jeeps pull up outside, all matt black and ominous-looking. Goddess knows what the neighbours are going to think.

We split up, as a single vehicle won't accommodate us all. Which concerns me — was that their intention?

I'm in with Jackson. His hand transmits warmth, energy and comfort, soothing my nerves and instilling a little more faith in myself and the others. We can handle this; we've been in far worse predicaments, after all.

We arrive at our destination in record time; these

guys don't hang about. The roads were clear and we jumped several red lights; they obviously pre-arranged this to allow us through without delay. I think I squeezed all the blood out of Jackson's hand. I realise that it's his arrival in my life that's making me more nervous than I'd been before. Previously, I had little regard for my safety and future, but now I'm terrified of losing him so soon after we've found each other.

'You won't get rid of me that easily,' he whispers to me, knowing instinctually what I need to hear.

I believe him, and it was nice to hear.

The airfield is essentially an overgrown piece of land enclosed by trees, a heavily weathered, fractured strip of tarmac running through the centre, with a dilapidated shack and small tower overseeing proceedings. There wasn't a news van in sight.

The people who transported us? I'm reluctant to refer to them as the regular army; they could have been special forces? It's hard to tell; you put someone in a nondescript black uniform and hand them a machine gun and they lose all individuality.

They weren't very forthcoming with information, either; the only words I could pry out of any of them were: 'You'll be briefed upon arrival at the site, miss.'

Briefed! They knew nothing, that's what it boiled down to. And "miss"? I didn't know whether to be flattered or insulted.

Anyway, we all arrived together and intact. I

noticed a few stares, mostly directly at Ix, as we disembarked and regrouped; but their interest was soon quelled when Nikki stepped up beside her and flashed them a toothy smile. Goddess knows what they made of that.

Besides which, we do emanate a certain kind of energy. I do take it for granted sometimes; I forget, due to the fact I isolate myself from society a great deal of the time, unlike Maddie and Nikki, who took all this in their stride, and Kal had such a confident air about her — nothing seemed to faze her. And, obviously, Sophia got a few appreciative looks; the downside to being beautiful, I suppose.

Life's so hard!

But our combined aura seems to attract good souls and repels bad ones. I can't put it more succinctly than that. And since we returned from that hellish realm, all our powers have increased; it's so much more potent, and as a result, I did notice a few sweaty, uncomfortable individuals amongst our escort.

A few dark secrets and troubled consciences?

The helicopter was already waiting for us, big and black. Wouldn't it hurt them to use a little colour here and there? It's not as if black blends into the blue sky. Unless they're out at night; then again, they could have blue ones for daytime jaunts.

You're babbling again, Alice! Sorry, nerves.

'Sikorsky CH-53.'

Thanks, Deek, not that I really needed to know that.

There was ample room for us all, and we were quickly strapped in. I watched on as the poor soul tasked with Maddie's security fumbled at the straps as she stared unflinchingly at him through those mirrored lenses. But he completed his task and almost fell out of the door in his haste to retreat.

These people are actually scared of us. The majority of them, at least. I did catch a couple of friendly smiles, directed towards Kal, and a friendly wave or two, as the engine burst into life and the rotor blades commenced their rotation.

The escort didn't hang around once we'd been safely delivered, and were already departing by the time we lifted off.

I'd never been in a helicopter before, and I don't intend on repeating the experience if I can possibly help it.

Did I mention I hate heights?

'Ha!' Maddie exclaimed, as we flew low over a small town, at the few early commuters who were on the move at this hour.

Despite the breaking dawn, she could see quite clearly; although not gifted with the same night-time capabilities as Nikki, she does have remarkable sight.

'These mortals in their vehicles are even more insignificant from up here.'

'Yes, they appear as insects,' Nikki agreed.

I dread to think how those meetings they've been attending play out with that kind of attitude. They were incorrigible. And goddess knows what the two in the cockpit were thinking if they could hear their conversation.

'There are many good and worthy souls amongst their number,' Ix defended them. She approached this new mode of transportation with her usual open-mindedness and child-like awe.

Kal nodded firmly in agreement, arms folded — just the two!

'I jest with you,' Maddie responded. 'But many more have hearts as black as night.'

'And I have tasted much of that darkness.'

Don't start talking about draining people of blood, Nikki; I don't think my stomach could take it.

'Och, what you're needin' is a guid night out in Glasgae; that'd sort ya oot.'

I think they struggle with Deek's Scottish twang much of the time. I'm used to it, and Jackson has never had issues with language barriers.

'Glasgae?'

It sounds strange on Nikki's lips.

'Glasgow,' I clarify for her.

'Is this a place I should visit?'

'Och, aye.'

'Perhaps I shall, then, upon our return, and taste of the locals.'

I shake my head in despair. Needless to say, Deek and Anastassia have never been informed of her dietary requirements. The fewer people that know, the better.

'Sweet. I hope ya' can hud your drink, lassie, cos when I get in the zone, I can drink fa Scotland.'

Nikki gives one of her little smiles before answering. 'Oh, I can drink, have no fear of that.'

Is this conversation really happening?

I check on the others. Sophia has her eyes half-closed. She's wrapped up in a thick cashmere sweater, staring blankly out of the window. She looks bored. Probably used to luxury accommodation; the nuts-and-bolts décor of the helicopter's interior will be a bit of a culture shock to her. She senses my scrutiny and gives me a warm smile. My nausea feels better already; maybe I should have squeezed in beside her? Never mind, it can't be much further. I notice Mist is rather quiet, though.

'You okay?'

'Of course. Why wouldn't I be?'

She's as scared as I am. I don't know if it's heights or flying itself, but she's pure white and she's holding very tightly onto Anastassia.

And in case you're wondering — are they an item? Well, what do you think? I'm saying no more.

'In Russia, our military had insufficient funding.'

Here we go, tales from the motherland. I usually love these stories once Anastassia gets going. But I'm not sure I want to hear this one right now.

'Our helicopters didn't have doors; they were removed and the metal smelted to make ammunition.'

Mist goes a little paler, if that's possible? You know what, I think I'll join her in a shade change!

'Even the harnesses were removed to make utility belts. You just had to hang onto the seat or your comrades.'

What?

'You must've lost a few buddies?' Deek laughs. 'Remember to pack your 'chute.'

'We weren't issued with parachutes; they were deemed unnecessary and too expensive. And yes, we did lose some comrades. You learn to develop a strong grip.'

Deek's eyebrows shoot up and I thank the goddess for military funding and doors.

'I remember once…'

Oh, no, she's not finished yet.

'One bench wasn't even attached to the fuselage. The bolts had been removed to repair some equipment, and when we banked hard the whole bench slid out. We lost three good soldiers that day.'

She delivered this in an emotionless "these things happen" kind of way. I can't believe she survived this long. If I get the opportunity in the future, I'll try to remember to tell you the one she told us about the Russian general who went deer hunting — in a tank! I kid you not. She should write these down in a memoir: "How I Survived My Life in the Military".

20

We landed as close to the famous stones as the amassed crowds would allow, amidst a drizzle of cold rain.

Now I recall why I hadn't spent more time in England.

'Och, I've always wanted to visit Stonehenge,' Deek commented, peering out of the window as we touched down.

Well, at least someone seems to be enthusiastic at being here.

'Lieutenant Briggs,' the soldier that met us as we disembarked introduced himself. He was young and nervous-looking.

'Lieutenant.' Jackson stepped up, offering his hand, which was grasped, clasped and released.

The Lieutenant's eyes lingered on Ix's face briefly, before he continued, 'Glad you could make it. If you would all follow me, we have a base of operations set up where you'll be debriefed.'

There's that word again, "debriefed". Typical pre-programmed military response.

He led us across a stretch of the field lined with military personnel and vehicles. I could hear the vigilant crowds beyond clamouring to see who had just been flown in.

The base of operations turned out to be a large mobile trailer. I don't know why I expected a tent? Then he stood aside to allow us entry.

'Let me take that for you.' He offered to relieve Kal of the bag she still carried.

She delivered him a stare in response that made him take a step back. He didn't ask again.

Despite Anastassia's and Mel's assurances that they had both kept the details of our sojourn to that place as vague as they could get away with, particularly regarding our talents, I was still concerned about what these people knew about us. After all, Hotdog, Sam and Sweets had witnessed first-hand what we were capable of and had presumably been successfully airlifted out of Saudi Arabia after we left. Still, perhaps their reports had also gained us a modicum of respect as well? I guess we'll find out soon enough.

The command unit is even more cramped than I expected, the interior stuffy and filled with the electronic hum of banks of equipment. I don't like it in here — it messes with my ability to focus — but Jackson reaches for my hand and I feel that comforting surge.

We were quickly ushered through the interior to the rear, where a small segregated office had been installed.

Seated behind a desk was a general. I'm guessing

he is anyway, judging by the large colourful palette pinned to his lapel. We squeezed in and the door was closed behind us.

He took a few seconds to complete a task on the laptop before him, before finally deigning to acknowledge us, staring at us with Benicio Del Toro eyes. He's an actor, if you didn't already realise. If you don't know him, then look him up online; you'll see what I mean about his eyes.

'So, this is the team that allegedly prevented a full-scale invasion of... monsters' — he chose his word carefully — 'from destroying countless innocent lives.' He sat back, outwardly unimpressed at what stood before him.

What was he expecting? A room full of seven-foot Arnold Schwarzenegger types?

'I must confess, if I hadn't seen the footage of some of these creatures myself, I'd find it very hard to believe.'

Despite this confession, you could hear the cynicism in his voice, and I could feel my team tense in resentment.

This was going well! It was getting hot in here, and I'm not just referring to the temperature.

'Jackson.' The general finally acknowledged one of us by name. 'It's good to finally meet you in person.'

So, Jackson's had some dealings with this idiot before?

'And you, general.'

I knew it wasn't; it was just enforced social protocol.

'Well, what can you tell us about this being?'

'We know as much as you, general.'

Good for you, Jackson, tell him nothing. Besides, what little we knew would've been of no benefit to him anyway. Everyone else remained silent, happy to allow Jackson to be our representative.

'We believe her intentions will be revealed once we make contact with her.'

Indeed, we couldn't even be sure that her intentions were hostile; she might just have dropped in to say "hi!"

Yeah, right!

The general raised an eyebrow. 'I'm not sure I can allow that.'

What? Then why the hell bring us here? The pompous old-windbag.

'You have no jurisdiction in this matter.'

I didn't think Nikki would remain quiet for much longer.

'Really? Miss…?'

Don't call her that. I can see this situation spiralling out of control quickly now.

'I am no miss! I am Nyx, and I have lived thousands of your pathetic and insignificant lifetimes, mortal!'

Here we go! I could see that coming a mile off.

The general, however, keeps his cool. 'Well.' A

small, barely disguised smirk plays on his lips. 'You'll forgive me if I find that very hard to believe. You didn't inform me, Jackson, that your team were deluded, and shall we say mentally unstable?'

'Aye, well, you'd better believe it, general.'

'Derek McCain, I believe?' The general plucked his name off a sheet on his desk.

'Ma friends call me Deek. You can call me Derek.'

Deek's response gives me a few seconds' thinking time. I've got to come up with something fast before the general finds himself on the wrong end of Nikki's fury, and I can feel it escalating. If this scenario had played out even just a year ago, he would be toast by now.

The general knits his fingers together. 'And a Russian military operative as well. Can't say that I'm entirely comfortable with that.'

'Ex-military,' Anastassia adds. 'I'm a civilian now.'

Please don't start on Anastassia, because Mist will be over that table quicker than the general can say "diplomatic immunity". And my patience has just run dry regarding this pompous ass-hole.

'General, my name's Alice. I'm sure it's printed on that little sheet in front of you. It's quite a simple decision. Either you allow us to tackle this problem for you, or you can give us all a lift back home. But that would be inadvisable. You don't know what you're dealing with here, and we have had experience with such things.' Well, not quite like what was standing outside waiting for us, but he didn't know that. 'We've tackled things that would make your hair turn white.'

'As white as marble.'

I throw Maddie a cold stare — not now!

'So, what's it to be, general? Because I've got better things to be doing and I haven't had my breakfast yet.' I hadn't; I just can't eat that early in the morning.

He ponders for a moment, singling out Sophia. 'A world-renowned fashion model? Not the kind of publicity I was hoping for.'

'You already have all the publicity you could expect. Have you seen the television coverage?' Kal wades in, leaning heavily on his desk to stare him directly in the eye. 'In case you hadn't noticed, probably every television set in the world is tuned in to this small piece of England. You would do well to think hard about the decision you are about to make. Perhaps if you spent less time protecting your own best interests and allowed us to do our job, then the sooner we can all go home.'

'You have to understand that I am only an elected representative. The situation is far more convoluted than any of you understand.'

I think I'm getting the gist of it. If Maria's alien origins turn out to be legitimate, then there are going to be a lot of interested parties who are going to be queuing up for a piece of that armour after this. The highest bidder wins, then the restructuring of their military begins, and that's worrying — or would they justify it as defence?

But back to our current situation. Enough is enough, I'm going in.

'Perhaps a little demonstration, general?' I've been practising. Whereas my skills are mainly in conjuration and manipulation, Jackson's is more focus and application. But together we can achieve so much more.

I focus my intent and manipulate the conjured energy, and hey presto! The general's laptop is now a compressed cube of metal and plastic.

I can tell by Nikki's smile that she rather enjoyed that.

'That was an expensive laptop.'

'I'm sure the people you represent will have a whip-round for a new one.'

'You'll no' get much porn on that now, general!' Deek informs him.

The general throws him a dark look, but refrains from rebuking him. He quickly composes himself and eyes us all once more, a little more warily this time, I feel.

'If you can spare a tank, I'll make you a nice paperweight.' Not sure if I could actually perform that, but he's not aware of that. I wouldn't mind giving it a go, to be honest.

He finally gets to his feet, a look of weary

resignation on his face.

One-nil to team Alice!

'Come with me.'

He opens a door at the rear of the tiny office and leads us back outside. The feel of the cool drizzle on my face is so refreshing after being cooped up in there with the puppet general.

Dawn is well in ascendancy now and bands of pale orange and violet are slowly dispersing as the sun climbs, giving us all a clearer view of Maria as we approach. She's even more imposing in real life.

Above the ring of stones, we can easily discern her torso, making her at least thirty-five feet in height. The rising sun glistens off that golden carapace, giving it a warm, almost molten-looking consistency. Above that ring of stones, her torso displays her feminine curves, and her head and arms have cannula running across the surface: possibly some sort of hydraulic system to aid her movement or convey energy or fluids. I don't know. I'm guessing now, just trying to relate to you what my first impressions are. But one thing's for sure: the television doesn't do justice to the sheer majesty of her presence.

Her eyes glow with an unearthly quality, casting shadows over the rest of her face, making any further details hard to establish, except for a coronet of spikes or antennae. Whether a communications array or an indication of her sovereignty, I'm unsure, but she just radiates power and intelligence, and I get a distinct feeling that she's scrutinising us.

'She is aware of our presence. She has been awaiting our arrival.' Sophia confirms my suspicions.

The general casts her a look, but does not comment.

First, we are led to a tent — had to be one somewhere — pitched just outside the outer perimeter of the stone circle.

The military and their guns! The interior is brightly lit with LEDs revealing everything the taxpayers' money has to offer.

'If you require any ordnance, then now's the time to speak up.'

I'm not buying it this time, but Anastassia and Mel accept the general's offer. The rest of the team also abstain.

'So, we've been given the go-ahead, then?' Jackson enquires.

The general taps his ear. 'I've been given an affirmative.'

'We were being monitored back there?' I ask, and immediately wish I hadn't. Of course we were; it would be standard procedure under the circumstances. And now they've got some lovely shots of us all.

'The people I represent were very impressed with your little display back there.'

I give myself a metaphorical admonishing slap on the head for that. How stupid was that? Now I'm kind of thinking that that whole meeting was orchestrated specifically to provoke some sort of reaction. And I gave them it! Now, I'm remembering our helicopter departing as we were conducted to the command trailer. And the two batons those privates are armed with; "sick-sticks", I think I've heard them called.

I'm getting a horrible feeling that when we successfully deal with Maria — if we successfully deal with Maria — the general and his entourage aren't going to whisk us back home with a congratulatory pat on the back and a cheery wave. Instead, I'm seeing isolation cells and people in white coats brandishing scalpels and syringes... Stop it, Alice! You're freaking yourself out.

I feel a double-squeeze where Jackson still holds my hand. He's aware, too; at least if we all stick together, then they're going to have a hard time containing us; then there's the media coverage.

Jackson gives me a little wink and Nikki delivers me one of her smiles. Chill, Alice, and have a little faith, we've got this. You know, maybe a stone general stood beside my bear would look pretty cool? That's if I don't squash him into a small ball of putty before Maddie whips her shades off.

Just one act of aggression, general... the ball's in your court now.

Both Anastassia and Deek choose rather efficient-looking weapons with attached grenade launchers. I must admit, I'm a bit tempted. My previous obsession regarding flamethrowers comes to mind, but I resist — Maria's outer casing would no doubt repel such an obvious attack. She is, after all, Nephilim, so I have my doubts regarding the overall effectiveness of anything the general can offer at this stage. Even a nuclear strike. I could imagine, after the dust settles, Maria still standing there unscathed, surrounded by scorched chaos.

'EMP grenades?' Deek asks.

He's directed to a container, and Deek helps himself.

Electro-Magnetic Pulse grenades? Perhaps Deek is onto something there. Good luck to him.

Jackson gives my hand a squeeze and a tiny shake of his head, just in case I'm tempted. What does he know? I focus and pick up a scenario where we are shot after the event, mistaken for terrorists by the army. The spin doctors could certainly sell that synopsis to the already paranoid masses. But unarmed musicians? Well, that would be a far trickier sell.

Maddie points to the bulge beneath the general's jacket. 'I'll take that one. And, general, that is not negotiable.' Her determined tone and disconcerting mirrored stare see that the general complies. Unenthusiastically would be an understatement. And she accepts it as he hands it over.

Good call. We all know she doesn't want it or need

it, but it was merely intended to disarm him.

Maddie checks there's a bullet in the breech, before tucking the heavy gun in her belt. 'I'll try not to lose it, general.'

I can see him bite at his lip as he catches himself and refrains from responding. I'm betting he hasn't been spoken to like that for a long time. Well, it's long overdue.

Kal has unpacked her blades and Mist's axe and they've secured them in place.

We're finished here.

At least it's stopped raining. The grass is still heavy with moisture, the light covering of cloud is slowly dissipating in the wind that is now picking up, making it seem colder than it is.

I've never been to Stonehenge before and I'm immediately impressed by the sheer scale of the structure. You should visit — not now, obviously, it's really busy.

We gather beneath one of the huge trilithons — I believe that's what they're called — and I gaze up at Maria in wonderment. So, this could be the very source of humankind's emergence on this planet. Our true creator, a god.

I've got to admit I'm feeling very inconsequential at the moment; both physically and spiritually.

There are three or four science heads scurrying about like mice between us and the inner collection of stones, where Maria stands unresponsive to their administrations, as they take readings with various instruments and video footage of the golden goliath for posterity.

'We can take it from here, general,' Anastassia informs him.

'Unless ya fancy steppin' in the ring wi' us, of course?' Deek adds playfully.

We all turn to him, awaiting his decision. He scowls, and it's a good scowl. He should grow a bushy moustache so he can wobble his upper lip as well when he's scowling, and maybe mutter under his breath: "Damn pesky kids!"

'Twonk!' Deek adds, as the general finally retreats, just loud enough for him to hear.

I just presumed at the time that "twonk" was some Scottish form of derogatory insult. But I looked it up and it's a proper word.

So, without even deliberating on the subject, Deek has inadvertently provided you with a new word for the day — twonk — meaning a stupid or foolish person. How appropriate.

I like it. I shall endeavour to use it more in conversation.

Right, Maria. I don't know how to approach this at all.

'Should we attempt to communicate with her first?'

We scoot to one side as the boffins hasten out of the

arena.

'We will have to initiate some form of response. It would, therefore, be sensible to approach her with caution, but also peacefully; we still can't be sure that she wishes to cause us or anyone else any harm,' Ix puts forward.

'Agreed. She may just be here to observe,' Jackson adds.

'But observing what? A large deployment of military excess?'

I could see Anastassia's point; it wasn't much as far as welcoming parties go.

'This armour she wears appears to be designed for conflict,' Sophia concludes, studying the giant.

'I tend to agree with Sophia,' Nikki nods. 'There can be no other explanation for her outward appearance.'

'Wid she no' need a suit to travel through space?'

Nikki gives Deek a disparaging look.

'Och, I only asked.'

'The Nephilim do not travel through space. They exist beyond the veils of creation,' Sophia adds by way of an explanation.

Hope that helped, Deek!

We step into open ground between the two rings of stone; there seems little reason to prevaricate further.

I'm suddenly very aware of being scrutinised by her and the millions, quite possibly billions, all over the globe. Is this what it must feel like walking out on stage in front of thousands of screaming fans? Suddenly, I'm relieved I didn't insist on taking up the position of lead vocalist.

The sun, still low on the horizon, is peeking through the scurrying clouds, and the light strikes Maria's armour. It seems to glow as if absorbing the solar energy, and it occurs to me that she may have been recharging her batteries all this time.

I can't make out any joints on the epidermal layer, and I get the sensation that this is like skin, a living organism, but without any of the usual biological features: fingernails; nipples; navel. Then again, were the Nephilim subject to the usual ways of reproduction that we as humans were? I doubt it.

We spread out and form a semi-circle before her. Without the general's unwanted proximity, we take up positions without the aid of the spoken word. We're working harmoniously now. We know what's required.

I'm sticking close to Jackson. Clasping of hands isn't required — his presence and that of the rest of the team is all that's called for now to focus and magnify my power.

Anastassia and Mel keep the muzzles of their rifles lowered, for now; we can't be seen to be the antagonists here.

Here goes nothing. 'Can you hear us? Do you wish to communicate something to us?' I feel ridiculous as I speak the words, and we wait patiently for a response.

She's not very chatty.

The seconds seem to stretch; nothing... no, wait. Her eyes are glowing more intensely now, getting brighter. As if someone restoked a furnace behind that mask, the light flares up and that mighty head shifts to stare down upon us.

The next few seconds pass inordinately quickly.

I feel the atmosphere shift as she emits a twin pulse of light, emanating from her eyes.

It's powerful and I'm temporarily blinded and disorientated. I stagger back a couple of paces, throwing up a shield in an attempt to block any further attacks, but I'm not even sure that was what that was.

My sight is returning, and no further barrage of light is transmitted, so I chance a look to check on the predicament of my team, only to discover that I'm alone — they've completely vanished.

Or is it me that's vanished? Because not only have my friends disappeared, but so has Stonehenge. I've been completely transported somewhere else, somewhere I recognise — I'm back home, on my property in Canada.

What the...?

21

I can feel the rich loamy earth beneath my feet and smell the fresh tang of that pinewood forest in the air. Well, if this is an hallucination implanted in my brain from that light pulse Maria delivered, then it's a very convincing one.

But I'm not entirely alone. Maria's here as well, or a shrunken version of her, at least. I say that, but she's still got a foot and a half on me.

She's just standing there again, studying me, like she's waiting for me to make the next move.

What the hell is going on?

I slowly start to back up, keeping her firmly in my sights. As I retreat, she moves forward. Her pace is languid, confident, her movements fluid. Her eyes begin to glow again with that unearthly light. I know what's coming.

I halt in my tracks and form a sphere of protection around myself. The burst of energy she emits collides with the barrier I've erected and throws me back with incredible force, smashing me into the stone bear behind me.

That hurt! If it hadn't been for my shield, I

would've sustained an injury, possibly even a broken back or crushed skull. This isn't good; no conversation, no negotiation — just full-on attack mode. What is this about? Did we provoke her somehow? Is this retribution for killing Her or God Himself? Maybe they're related somehow? Hell, I don't know. Without some sort of explanation, I'm totally at a loss as to what this is about.

I pull myself up and Maria unhurriedly closes the gap between us. Those eyes start to fire up again.

Not this time! I've got an idea.

I form my intention and lift that stone bear at my back. Jackson has tutored me well. The statue arcs high above my head and I bring it back down to earth hard directly on top of Maria, flattening her.

I cautiously edge forwards in time to witness the fingers on one protruding arm stretch and clench, before ceasing all movement. Then the arm, and presumably the rest of her, simply dissolve into thin air.

'Nice one, Yogi.'

Then that flash of light again and I'm back at Stonehenge. This time the inner circle is filled with armed soldiers, milling about in a rather confused fashion, until I make a reappearance. Now they've got something to focus on — great!

I'm the only one here. The rest of the team and giant Maria are absent — double great!!

'Don't shoot!' I'd better be cautious here; these guys seem a bit too frisky. And here comes general hard-ass. 'Before you ask, general, I'm still trying to piece this together myself.'

Just as he opens his mouth to retort, Maddie appears at my side. I've never been so glad to see her.

'I need to know where that threat is. Or did you and your team conspire to relocate her to a secret location?'

The general's not too happy, and the impressive collection of guns are now pointed at myself and Maddie. I caution her with a small shake of the head as I see her fidget with her shades.

'My adversary has been satisfactorily dealt with, general,' she divulges, lowering her hand. 'And I lost your gun,' she adds, smiling.

'And what exactly does that mean?'

But before either of us could answer — not that either of us was in a very co-operative mood, with all those gun barrels pointed in our direction — Deek made a timely reappearance.

Now, over the next few minutes or so, the rest of the team did make it back, popping into existence one by one. So, I'll take this opportunity to visit each of their personal experiences as they happened; then we can re-join the current predicament live from Stonehenge — maybe we should do a gig here? Because that's got kind of a ring to it.

Let's take them in order, then: Maddie.

Her relocation experience was pretty much the same as mine: slight disorientation, then faced with a smaller version of Maria.

Her environment, judging by her description, sounded like a Mediterranean island, or something similar. She described a hot, desolate, rocky landscape punctuated with Greek-style columns and scrubby grasses. As far as I could make out, then, Maria had plucked some sort of setting directly from our memories. One which was familiar to us in some way, which was very peculiar. Surely an unconventional backdrop would give her an advantage over us?

Maddie explained that despite her very alien appearance, beneath that exoskeleton was a being, and very much alive. But not anymore. Well, that was that no further explanation required. And then, like myself, she found herself transported back here.

Deek found himself in Sauchiehall Street, Glasgow, but:

'The place was empty, like just afore dawn on a Sunday, ye ken, after all the bam pots had staggered hame!'

Well, if you can picture that, you're more informed than me. Same situation: small Maria, dispatched with his full quota of four EMPs.

'Wasnae takin' any chances,' as he put it, but it worked, as his return confirmed.

This whole plot was getting curiouser and curiouser.

Next was Kal, blue and armed to the teeth. I thought

the general was going to "leg it" cartoon style, legs spinning as they attempted to gain some traction on the damp ground. I think the distinct sound of safety catches being released stayed his flight. I noticed him lift a hand ever so slightly as a couple of soldiers looked to him for orders, and they held fire.

I had secured us all within a shield, invisible to all but me. I can faintly see it now, like a heat shimmer, which is a new addition. But whether it would repel that many bullets if he gave the command was something I'd rather not put to the test.

Needless to say, Maria wasn't sword-proof, or at least against Kal's enchanted demon-slayers. Her setting was within the confines of an Indian temple, the air heavy with burning incense — very homey.

This just seemed to be a little too easy. I'm thinking back to when we confronted Him. So, was there some other hidden agenda behind all this? Was there something worse on its way? Was this just some sort of test, before a full-scale invasion was launched?

And, more immediately, was the general waiting until we had all returned before giving the signal to open fire?

I casually reached out and clasped Maddie's hand. I was preparing for the worst-case scenario. We'd done this on enough occasions now that all present knew what the score was, and we were all soon linked together, Kal very slowly sheathing her armoury before reaching for Deek's hand, much to the relief of the soldiers.

Jackson was next, thank the goddess! He moved in on my other side, rather bemused by the sequence of events that were playing out in the circle.

What must the people be thinking at home? Best television ever, right?

Our holding hands was, fortunately, only seen as a pathetic show of solidarity and camaraderie by the general. I could tell by his body language and that smug smile.

He thought he had us — dream on.

Anyway, Jackson found himself not at home, but at Cambridge itself, in the very lecture room he had delivered his presentations. That was a period in his life when he had felt most content (until we met, of course), sharing his passion for knowledge with those of similar minds. And Maria? Crushed like a tin can. It was Jackson that taught me that, too; that was the first time I'd attempted it properly on the general's laptop. Jackson's a lot better at it than me.

Mist joined us next, having been transported onto a battlefield.

'That was her first and last mistake,' she commented. Valkyries, as you know, have the power to decide who will live and who will die on the battlefield.

I think Mist had the easiest challenge; she simply decided the outcome. She didn't even get to unsheathe her axe! She read the situation immediately and linked in.

There were a few minutes' delay before the next arrival. I'll admit I was getting a bit anxious by the time Ix put in an appearance.

Ix had to rely on direct contact to overpower her version of Maria. Arriving in a jungle environment, she had to "ghost" her way behind Maria, which wasn't as easy as it sounded. Even in ghost-mode, Ix was still susceptible to Maria's energy blasts, and it took her several attempts to successfully outmanoeuvre her and finally take hold of her golden cranium, helmet, I'm not sure what you'd call it.

Ix told me that the helmet flowed with life beneath her fingers, but unlike any form of life she had yet encountered. Which confirmed Maria's alien origins. But life is life, whatever its form, and Ix successfully shut down her motor functions and… well, here she is.

It was another few minutes, before Anastassia turned up. Looking rather hot and bothered, it looked like she'd been working out.

Back home in Russia, on the banks of a lake where she used to go to escape the attentions of her stepfather, Maria had proved to be bullet-proof and grenade-proof. Typical! So, Anastassia had had to engage in a game of cat and mouse, hence her appearance. She knew the area well, though, and it was exactly how she had remembered it as a child. But inevitably Maria caught her, Anastassia stumbling over a rock.

'I had given up, it was time to finish this, I couldn't keep running forever, I would face my death with dignity. She grabbed me by the throat, her eyes glowing like the devil himself. I could feel her fingers closing on my throat; she intended to throttle me. I did the only thing I had left, the only thing I could think of.' She held up her prosthetic here and made a fist. 'I punched through that golden armour into her chest. She let go and I punched her again and again. She is finished.'

You could indeed see the bruises around her throat where Maria had had a hold of her. Anastassia had had a lucky escape. Or was it? I just couldn't shake the feeling that this was some sort of test.

I was on the edge of my seat when Anastassia later related her experience; she has a way about her when she tells a story that enthrals you.

I was rather surprised that Sophia hadn't shown up by now, but she made a rather timely arrival after Nikki, who was next.

Nikki had to go one better and had brought back a souvenir. The severed golden head she clutched was thrown at the general's feet. It then vaporised as quickly as it increased in size. 'A gift for you, general,' she mocked.

Later on, she revealed she had simply twisted it off. What?

Her shadow form had rendered any strike by Maria

futile, which had allowed Nikki to get close enough to decapitate her. When I asked where she was, she just replied that it was dark. 'A darkness that coincided with creation.' Very enigmatic — so a torch might have been in order; well, thinking of myself.

Maybe there was something in that: the most ancient of us having no quandary about how to deal with this Nephilim? But still, couldn't this being try harder? Her futility almost seemed sacrificial.

I noticed, as Nikki joined our line, that the general had given the soldier nearest him a certain look. Jackson squeezed my hand as well. This was happening. Jackson knew better than any of us — well, certainly better than me — what was going on in that repellent little military mind of his.

But I was good to get us the hell out of there as soon as Sophia showed up. I could feel Jackson focusing; it was almost like his mind was somehow superimposed upon mine, and he was letting me know his intentions. If the general gave the order to fire those weapons, they would be so much compressed metal. But he was holding back until the first move was made; we were the protagonists here, we weren't going to stoop to the level of the general. And faced with so many guns, the energy that would be required by Jackson to successfully render them all useless may result in one or more of the troops being injured or worse; and that was something he wanted to avoid at all costs, for all our sakes.

I already had the image of home imprinted in my head — home Canada, that is, not London. The general and his troops would be swarming all over that place like flies in no time, if they weren't already.

Sophia arrived in a blaze of divine light. Quite a breathtaking arrival, I have to admit; much better than Maria's sudden materialisation at Stonehenge. Either way, divine beings certainly know how to make an entrance.

Maria was easily dispatched by Sophia's sword within the— 'pastures of ambrosial repose'. Sounded rather nice, I thought, wherever that is — could be a retirement home on the Dorset coast somewhere?

She had delayed her return to watch over us and ensure our safety before coalescing. Her powers are still very much of a mystery to me, and her glowing, six-winged full-Seraph mode commanded a certain adoration.

Gun barrels dropped, as did jaws; even the general switched his attention to this apparition of heavenly exquisiteness.

Nice one, Sophia; now time to get us out of there faster than a penguin down a water chute.

The image of home intensified as Sophia linked in, all present still gazing in wonderment, until Deek broke the spell just before we translocated.

'Hey, general,' he called, and pulling Kal's hand up so he could deliver his message, he flipped him the middle finger.

The picture on the general's face was absolutely priceless.

22

Needless to say, upon our return we were in full DEFCON 1 mode; or at least I was. Fully anticipating a hostile invasion force of armed-to-the-teeth commandos.

Well, it never happened.

Deek informed me that the weapons those soldiers had aimed at us were tranquilliser guns. I couldn't tell the difference; when you're staring down the barrel of a gun, they all look the same to me.

They were state of the art, a new design. But Deek had encountered them before in Nicaragua — some of the special forces' guys stationed there had been testing their effectiveness in the field. Which means all my earlier fears weren't just paranoia; the general had indeed intended to take us in for study.

Which made perfect sense, when there was no guarantee that regular bullets would actually kill us, and then throw away the opportunity to replicate and weaponise our abilities. Although I'm pretty sure tranquillisers wouldn't have worked on the majority of us anyway — just really annoyed them.

Maddie gave me an amused look when she spotted

the bear on his back well and truly embedded in the earth.

'I had to improvise.'

'So I see.'

That did raise the question about whether our individual experiences had been real or illusion. Very much real, then.

We kept things very tight over the next few days, and if they had turned up with the intention of drugging us and carting us off, well, it was gloves off.

Even Deek, who had returned still armed with his assault rifle, had no qualms now about defending us.

It was Sophia's attendance at the scene in the end that I think was our saving grace; our very own guardian angel.

Initially, the media coverage of the event had been heavily censored by the military, claiming technical problems. But they still made the mistake of filming the entire incident; from our arrival, our unexpected disappearance — including that of Maria — and then our return and miraculous vanishing act.

Well, you can guess. Whether it was leaked by military personnel or by some bystander lucky enough to capture it on their phone, an event as momentous as the manifestation of an angel was bigger news than the alien robot.

It took twenty-four hours for the footage to make it onto the internet and go global. We were now internationally famous and saviours of humankind.

There's no going back now.

This kind of phenomenon is going to certainly give the church something to mull over, that's for sure. And change many people's outlooks and ways of life. I mean, after witnessing this, would people now question the whole aspect of heaven and hell? And could they be condemned to an existence of eternity in the underworld unless you lived a virtuous life?

I think it must have been the deciding factor regarding the military's pursuit of us as well. You can't shoot down and experiment on a real-life angel; that would be blasphemous, wouldn't it?

That footage was a turning point for humankind, and too many people had been physically present on-site for any hope of casting it off as fake news.

All down to Sophia — bless her!

But we still had the problem of Maria — wait, isn't that a song from something? — and what her visitation had implied. I've already shared with you several of my theories and dilemmas surrounding her unexplained arrival, but none of them rang true for me.

The only definite detail we had was that she had been waiting for our arrival. So much so that I did wonder, if we hadn't shown up, would she still be standing there? She would have certainly given the druids something to ponder over and dance around at the solstice. But then again, would she have eventually come hunting for us?

Who am I kidding? The military would have stepped in and goddess knows how that would have ended?

Was it all, in fact, a test? Should we now be expecting a full legion of Marias to descend upon us? Nikki put forward the idea that her presence had been a gift, allowing us to gain confidence as individuals as well as within the team itself.

Hmm? I wasn't convinced, either. Unless, of course, the whole demonstration had been contrived in order to divulge our true identities, pushing humankind forward on that spiritual path. Could the Nephilim be that implicated in humankind's continued existence and development?

Ix said something interesting which tied in with what I had experienced and seen when she had gifted me with that insight into the afterlife. Now that conditions had been rectified for the advancement of the human soul, our intervention had set off a chain reaction; we had essentially been catalysts. A small link in the chain had been established and now we could allow life, and death, to progress as it was always intended.

I don't know about you, but I quite liked this explanation. The thought that these divine beings were watching over us and manipulating events and people — or, as I like to think, "guiding" — to aid in our evolution.

But wow! Right? This was colossal, life-altering stuff! I much preferred Ix's view than the idea that was put forward that the Nephilim were merely bored and recognised in us a challenge. The same sort of challenge a hunter might express when stalking his or her prey, and it was just sport to them. Perhaps? But for now, I'm going with the other one.

But to be honest, no-one knew for sure; after all, they were essentially beings from another dimension, real-life aliens, so could anyone really be expected to fathom correctly what they were truly thinking? So, who knows, presumably aliens have alien ways and we'll just have to accept that and move on. And if they return? Well, we'll deal with that if it happens.

Enough! All this speculation is giving me a headache. And I haven't even touched upon the subject of what their world and others may be like in reality. As Deek put it — 'Do ya think it's like in that film wi' the talkin' raccoon?'

I don't know? I don't even know what the hell he's talking about. I don't see what relevance talking animals has on any of this?

But now it's on to the good stuff…

Postlude

The captured footage was played incessantly on the television until it got to the point where I didn't want to switch it on. But my favourite bits were Nikki tossing the severed head at the general, and, of course, Sophia's spectacular arrival. Oh, and, of course, Deek, flipping the general the finger. Classic! Have you seen the T-shirts yet?

Deek bought one himself. It's weird seeing him wearing a T-shirt depicting an image of himself with the slogan — "we came, we saw, we kicked alien ass!" I'm going to lose that in the wash unless he escapes with it back to Glasgow first.

Now that our secret identities had been revealed in true superhero style, what now?

Well, first off, there was Sophia's farewell modelling gig, which, as it was in New York, we decided we couldn't miss the occasion. And we had to make a public appearance, didn't we? It was going to happen sooner or later anyway.

And what a night it turned out to be!

Kal kept a low profile, though, and I implemented my magical filters to aid her in her disguise. Until later that night, that was.

And Sophia: what a performer; as she took her final sashay down the catwalk, she took a moment to survey the cheering crowd, before unravelling her six wings and going Seraph. I thought the roof to the venue was going to lift off! I think I had a religious experience myself; or was that later with Jackson?

We partied into the early hours and much of the following day. Turns out Deek can drink; and as it happens, so can Nikki, and I'm not just talking about the red stuff, either! Although I do seem to remember them on red wine at some point. I even indulged myself, so my memory of events is a bit hazy. But they've become firm friends now. Who could have called that? Maddie, too. So, they've now become the terrible trio!

I recall the three of them, arm in arm, singing Frank's "That's Life"; now that was a sight to behold. I'm sure someone filmed it, so you'll be able to check it out online for yourself. Plus, the countless selfies of Kal, all blue and multiple-limbed. I've never seen her so buoyant, now finally freed from the constraints her image had placed upon her.

And, wait for it, Mist and Anastassia got engaged!
Mind is officially blown!

There's a big age difference, of course, not that you'd notice. It's mind-numbing when you think about it, but there are ways around that. A mortal can join the ranks of the immortals, apparently; I do seem to recall that during my brief study of Greek myth, so it's all good.

Ix has become some kind of holy woman, a dispensary of wise words, soother of troubled souls and balm to distressed minds. If they had more like her employed within the mental health sector, then we'd, at last, be seeing some positive progress. And she loves it, said that she'd spent such an aeon of time with the dead, it was such a gift to be surrounded by so much life. There's no arguing with that.

But despite all the revelations, it was undoubtedly Sophia's night, delighting her adoring fans by taking to the wing and then swooping in low, skimming the crowd. And why not? What was the point in hiding ourselves away now? And now that we're global, it offers a kind of protective shield to us, one which I couldn't compete with.

Any military, or other factions, for that matter, would find it virtually impossible to make a move on us now with the kind of crowds we were pulling. Just the slightest iota of negativity or aggression flaunted in our direction, especially Sophia's, and there'd be riots.

And speaking of crowds, the details of the tour literally took care of themselves and was an immediate sell-out. And the album's been at the top of the charts since recent events went public.

We're already cutting new material for a second album just before we head out on the road.

I'll have to leave you in a moment, constant companion. Duty calls: I can hear the unmistakable opening guitar licks to "Thunderstruck"; that's our call to arms — band practice time. One final recitation before we take it to the stage.

We'll have to cover that track, maybe close the show with it?

I'm sure what we've got planned will blow everybody's minds. What a show it's going to be. Angelic lead vocals, with myself (I've been persuaded) and Ix on backing. Anastassia's thumping bass rhythms and Mist playing that axe — I just knew she'd be awesome. And hold onto your hats. All those drummers that have been hailed the best over the decades? Well, take a back seat, six-arms, no competition, the studio album doesn't do her justice. And then there's the planned stage show itself, courtesy of myself and Jackson; magical — quite literally.

Maddie, Nikki and Deek make an indispensable team. Preparing the show, including pretty much everything you could think of: security; transport; bookings; accommodation; merchandising. The list just goes on. Kal even brought on board some of her defence class students to help with the roadie work and extra security.

I still can't help getting a bit stressed and anxious about upcoming events, publicity, interviews, anything really, but Deek just steps in and holds his hands up —

'Hey, we've got this sorted.' Meaning himself, Nikki and Mads — that's what he calls Maddie now! I don't know how he manages it!

Someone's cranked up the volume; just as well I haven't got any neighbours out here! Yogi's back in pride of place — Kal and Nikki lifted him between them, although I reckon either one of them could have managed on their own. They moved him like he was made of polystyrene!

We take to the road in a week; I'm so excited. And already we've got venues booked for our European leg of the tour. Glasgow's already on the calendar. I promised Deek we'd do that one; maybe we'll see you there?

You should check us out if you're at a loose end; it would be good to see you if you can snap yourself up a ticket — they're pretty hot property, by all accounts. All ticket sales go to charity, by the way — Amnesty International — it's not as if we need the money. The record sales alone more than cover the cost of the tour and the wages of all the extra staff we require to get this show on the road. We may be superhuman, but we still have our limitations.

Oh, yes, and Ix asked if we could donate merchandise sales to the WWF. She loves nature; been so out of touch with it for so long. I'm annoyed with myself that I hadn't thought of that one. So that's a done deal.

Anyway, I've prattled on long enough, as I'm sure you've got things to be getting on with, and I'm not sure those speakers are going to take much more volume. But please do check us out if you can; the critics reckon we're pretty good. Actually, I think I'm letting my modesty get the better of me!

You may have even heard of us already - *Pariahs*.